JUST
FAMILY

JUST
FAMILY

Tonya Bolden

COBBLEHILL BOOKS
Dutton   New York

Library of Congress Cataloging-in-Publication Data
Bolden, Tonya.
     Just family / Tonya Bolden.
         p.   cm.
     Summary: Ten-year-old Beryl is fairly content with her life in
East Harlem in the 1960s, until she learns that her older sister is
really her half-sister and worries that her family will begin to
change.
     ISBN 0–525–65192–6
     [1. Sisters—Fiction. 2. Family life—Fiction. 3. Afro-
Americans—Fiction.]   I. Title.
PZ7.B635855Ju   1996   [Fic]—dc20   95–32876   CIP   AC

Published in the United States by Cobblehill Books,
an affiliate of Dutton Children's Books,
a division of Penguin Books USA Inc.,
375 Hudson Street, New York, New York 10014

Designed by Jean Krulis
Printed in the United States of America
First Edition   10   9   8   7   6   5   4   3   2   1

For Nelta . . .

my sister and best friend

There once was a little girl who could be quite contrary.
But her name wasn't Mary. And she knew nothing at all of
silver bells and cockleshells. Her world was jump-rope
games and airplanes made out of Popsicle sticks and
Bazooka gum bubbles, two-pieces thick. Her world was a
neighborhood that had changed from Little Italy to Spanish
Harlem and now, in these heady 1960s days, was known
more plainly as East Harlem, around where Black Power
preachers were making much noise and news, and where
folks were eager to hear freedom ring.
Loud.
But this little girl wasn't much fazed by such things as this.
All she knew was her small world, which really boiled down
to her small wants. To her, freedom was time to
play, and having her way. And she had a fair amount of
that, and a few good friends. And she had her family,
which she took for granted like she did the air.
So all was right in her world.
Until one midsummer night's eve when she discovered
something that spun her into being a little more contrary.
And wary.
For awhile.

1

Beryl was reading through the poem for the third time, straining to come up with something special to say—for just the right words to say how much she adored what she didn't understand.

While Beryl studied the poem, Randy studied her little sister.

Beryl was richly dark from so much sun, bony, and dying to be tall. She was sitting cross-legged at the head of her bed. Her bottom lip was tucked in tight. Her eyes roamed the sheet of paper.

Randy, lean and long, was stretched out on her bed, propped up on her elbow, head in her hand. Her lips were pursed—part smile, part smirk. "Don't get it, do you?" she nudged.

"Almost," Beryl mumbled. "And it really is . . . something!" she added with some perk, looking up and then back down at the poem.

"It's about—"

"No-o-o," Beryl whined. "Don't tell me. I can figure it out."

"Poetry isn't math. You don't figure it out. You *feel* it."

"Okay, okay, okay. Then just give me a few more minutes to finish *feeling* it."

Beryl looked up and past Randy to the window with her face in a scrunch as if she were trying to remember something. She was seeing but not taking in the view of the half dozen twenty-story buildings like hers that towered over the basketball courts, handball courts, small horseshoe amphitheater, and play parks alive with monkey bars, swings, sprinklers, and brightly painted stone animals Beryl and her friends rode for miles and miles on adventures in the wild, wild West, the plains of Africa, and any place else their imaginations could reach.

Right now, the only place Beryl's mind was taking her was around and around in circles as she came closer to feeling the poem and proving herself worthy of this honor. It was only in the last few weeks that Randy had been letting her see some of her poetry.

Randy flopped on her back, crossed her hands behind her head. "One . . . Two . . ."

"No, don't do that! You making me lose my place and what I was gonna say. Give me more time. And if you gonna count, do it to yourself—and to ten."

"Three," Randy whispered. "Four . . . It's about our summertimes."

"I knew that!" Beryl insisted.

"Did not!"

"Did too! I was just trying to figure out—I mean, I was just trying to *feel* how I knew it, is all."

"It's about playing Whist at Grandma's—" Randy began to explain.

"And keeping it a secret!" Beryl interrupted in an animated whisper. "So you better not let Ma and Daddy see this poem."

"Don't be so silly, and don't worry. Even if they do see it, I'll just let them think it's the stuff I imagine."

"But that'd be like lying. Better to just make sure they don't never see it."

"Not telling them Grandma's taught us to play Whist and Tunk and Pitty-Pat when all they think we know how to play is Old Maid is like lying, but you don't seem bothered by that."

"That's keeping a secret. That ain't the same as lying."

"But it's not telling the truth, the whole truth, and nothing but the truth so help you God."

Beryl's frown was one of confusion. Hers was a mind most comfortable with absolutes. Good or bad, true or false, sweet or sour, hot or cold, right or wrong.

She didn't take well to in-betweens. This had something to do with why she liked what she called "real colors": fire truck red, blue jay blue, green like grass in spring. She didn't understand the colors Randy favored—maroon, burnt orange and aqua, and a rainbow of pastels. These were only sort-of colors—sort of red, sort of orange, sort of blue. As for pastels, they were, well . . . colors waiting to be real.

Beryl liked everything clear and definite and sure. This was why her favorite summer month was July. So much of June was spent in school that the handful of days that belonged to summer vacation didn't feel like real summer-vacation time. As for August, no matter how bright and shining the sky, the smell of back-to-school haunted the air, darkness nibbled away at daylight a little bit sooner evening after evening, and store-window dummies were dressed up in plaids, corduroy, and itchy-scratchy wools, preparing for the autumn cool.

But July . . .

July was juicy, good-sweat hot, absolute and perfect summer. No thoughts of the school year behind or the one up ahead; no thoughts of anything except the sunup to sundown fun of ring-a-leerio, hot peas and butter, freeze tag, double Dutch, double orange, roller skating, black crow. And more and more, it was on the handball court that Beryl spent much of her time.

This July came with the added bonus of a trip Down South for a family reunion, not many days away. But at ten, even 'til tomorrow sometimes seems a forever wait.

Beryl thought her journey to the place her father called home would never come.

The big fun and adventure on her mind right now was the carnival. She could already hear it starting, and kept checking the clock, wishing it would hurry up and tick to 7:30. That's when her mother said they could go. Carnival week by itself was enough to make July precious; it meant having a little bit of Coney Island an elevator ride away. July had everything going for it.

Beryl thought it so weird that Randy's favorite month was November, which had nothing going for it but Thanksgiving. Sure, it meant a few days off from school, but there were no presents, just a lot of food. Too, the month was so in-betweenish. It didn't seem to fit in with either real fall or real winter.

Randy's taste in months was like her taste in colors. Beryl figured this had something to do with her wanting to be a poet and that thing she was always taking in her poems. Beryl couldn't remember what Randy called it right now. Poetic . . . lies, she thought, something like that.

Like this part of the poem about the steel drum and the basketball. She knew Randy was talking about that Jamaican man who'd sometimes turn up in the horse-shoe in the early evening with his funny, cratered drum and make smooth, lollipop-sounding music. As for the "basketball jones," she knew Randy was thinking about Tyrone, who took to the court solo late at night to practice foul shots and lay-ups by the light of the moon and the streetlamps splotching the walkways that snaked around the buildings. Randy was doing poetic lies when she put them two together, Beryl knew for sure. She'd never seen Jamaican Man and Tyrone doing their thing at the same time.

Beryl laughed at the sight of "Eye-talians." It looked just the way Grandma said it.

"So who are these saints!" she asked. "And why they going in circles? You trying to say that when the saints go marching in they're gonna be getting lost or something?"

"No, silly. Think. Think about crowds and confetti and Gina Conte's uncles."

"Oh, yeah. When the Italian people have that parade with the men carrying that big statue I bet Linda a dollar is going to fall down one day and—"

"Right. The Feast of Saint Anthony. The statue is him."

"So that's Saint Anthony? But how come you make it sound like there's lots of saints? It's only one."

"Poetic license," Randy huffed.

Oh, poetic *license*, Beryl said to herself.

"So, you get everything else?" Randy asked.

Beryl looked down at the poem again. "Yeah, I got everything else. It's about the good handballs that cost a quarter, only you spelled it the way we say it, because *nobody* says Spalding, but I guess that's some more of

6

your poetic lies—license." Beryl was feeling quite proud of herself. "And the fire hydrant holdups are when them bad boys break open the hydrants and make better sprinklers than we got in the park with soda cans." With a giggle, she added, "I just love it when they dare people in convertibles to drive on by."

Randy found herself enjoying Beryl's rundown on her poem more than she'd imagined she would.

"And then," Beryl continued, "it's about Fudgecicles, only all you say is that they're cool. And then it's about playing Pokeno, and then it's about, how we . . . those times when—"

"When we're—"

"No, don't tell me!" With a last fast glance at the poem, Beryl raced, "It's about listening to grownups talking about the olden days."

"Very good," Randy said in a teacher tone.

"And you named the poem after your favorite soda, Coco Rico, only you spelled it like it was chocolate," Beryl triumphed. "See-ee-e. I told you I got it!" Beryl was feeling even prouder now. "Can I read it out loud to you?" Before Randy could give the okay or the "No way," Beryl had cleared her throat and was off into—

COCOA RICO

A whist-ful Saturday night,
          hopin' to be
                    Trump-tight.

7

Deep into the night hearin' steel drummin'
keepin' time with somebody's
basketball jones.
saints goin' Round 'n' Round
on white-shoed Eye-talians with red bandannas.
and WE and the Ricans watch.
a 25¢ spal-deen fix and
fire hydrant holdups,
and lots of COOL fudgecicles.
And,
it was
SO hard to get corners—or was two of a kind
worse?
List'nin' to sagas of Greenwood and other Down South days and
how white folks used to be in
HARLEM!
all the time.

Randy applauded her with a soft patter clap. "Very good, very good. Rhonda wants me to read some of my poetry at Harambee House, you know. If you're nice to me, maybe I'll let you come and read that one."

"*Really?* Would you? When?"

"Oh, I don't know, whenever they have a poetry thing."

"I'll practice, I promise." Beryl would promise to do anything if Randy would take her to Harambee House. "But it'd be a whole lot easier to read if you wrote it straight. Why you put the words all over the page?

When Mrs. Pellegrino had us do poetry last year, she said every line had to be a sentence and start with a capital letter." As Randy heaved a heavy sigh of exasperation, Beryl squeezed in, "More poetic license, right? And you're trying to be like that man you and Rhonda are always talking about, aren't you? The one with the name that sounds like Abracadabra, and who puts a lot of cuss words in his poems. The one Ma said she'd better not never catch you reading again."

"Ashanti Bambara, stupid! And no, I'm not trying to be like anybody. I'm just being myself. You see, a poet—"

"Randy!" Beryl interrupted with a nod at the clock on the nightstand between their beds. "It's 7:30. Ma said we could go downstairs at 7:30!" When Randy rolled her eyes, she added, "You can finish telling me about your, you know, your poet ways in the elevator."

Randy really didn't feel like moving. She was not at all as enthusiastic about the carnival as Beryl, but she knew that if she didn't get ready to go right this minute Beryl would whine her to death. And anyhow, maybe I'll see Tyrone, she thought.

Beryl scrambled into her sneakers. Randy slipped into her sandals, and sauntered over to the vanity centered between their beds. She gave her hair a quick brush and pat. As she picked up her keys, Beryl shot, jackrabbit, from the room, and made the quick right into the entrance hall, yelling, "Okay, Ma, we're going now."

"Not so fast, girls," her mother called out from the kitchen, just as Beryl turned the front doorknob.

Aw, dag, Beryl sighed. What now?

"Remember, I want you upstairs by 9:30. Understood?"

"We will, Ma, don't worry. See ya later!"

"And I don't want y'all on the Ferris wheel, or that dinky roller coaster, or that other thing that flings you around in circles, you hear?"

Dag! Beryl sucked her teeth. That only leaves the slow-pokey kiddie rides.

"And I want you two to make sure you stay together. Randy, that means you keep an eye on your sister at all times. And Beryl, don't let me hear about you wandering off."

Isn't she ever going to forget about that?

"That" was last year when Mr. and Mrs. Nelson first let their daughters go down to the carnival by themselves. When Randy got caught up talking with some friends, Beryl spotted one of hers and skipped off. By the time Randy turned around and called out "Beryl!" her little sister was long gone into the crowd. After a short search, Randy went home in a panic only to find Beryl there, holding a humongous bucket of popcorn, which she said some strange man bought her, and telling her parents that Randy had lost her. Randy countered that Beryl had lost herself. Both girls got punished: Beryl for not staying with her sister, Randy for not being more watchful.

2

Beryl flew down the building's ramp and the stretch of concrete that sloped down to the sidewalk.

"Remember. If you don't stay with me I'm gonna tell," Randy shouted as she passed through the door.

"And I'll tell you still got Rhonda's book of poems by that Abracadabra man," Beryl shouted back. "Saw you reading it the other day, you know."

"So, go tell. See if I care," Randy shrugged from the top of the building's steps.

Beryl had no comeback for that. So she sucked her teeth, poked out her mouth, and stood where she was as Randy took her sweet time, exchanging "heys" and "what's hap'nins" with two girls entering the building.

Beryl soon abandoned her impatience as she took in the scene, as she yielded her whole self to her most prized place in the world: Outside.

The sounds of different musics crisscrossed and competed for her ears: all that brass of salsa from the building across the street; all that sass and soul of Martha and the Vandellas calling folks to come "Dancing in the Streets" from somewhere in the complex; and on a tinseled-up stage at one end of the block, the loud but limp sounds of some bleached-blonde women and skinny men in sparkly-spangly outfits doing no justice to "Heat Wave."

Somehow the sounds made a strange kind of harmony with the background music made by the people: that pounding hubbub of folks out for quick and easy fun on a night too hot to sleep; that zazzy blend of Spanglish and Southern drawls and Northern slick and throaty cool-speak and English Italian-style. There were children running wild and reckless through the crowd with squeals and shrieks and no shame. There were white and olive-skinned teenage boys sporting tattoos and jokes and winks and brags for girls named Rosita and Carmen and Chickie, girls who spied them out of the corners of their eyes, girls whose mothers would have killed them had they seen them with all that makeup on. There were light-brown and dark and deep dark-skinned boys jivin' and crackin' on each other and giving the up-and-down to girls named Adrienne and Shawnee and Brenda, girls with loud mouths and much "honey chile" and "ain't that a blip!"

Mingled in with the hubbub of this East Harlem crowd was the pierce of pinky-and-thumb whistles, the clap of hands slapping five, the mellow belly laughs, the giggles, the chuckles, the raucous hoots and howls. These lifenotes were jabbed by sudden shouts of gamesters luring folks to "Step right up!" and take a chance on winning something they never even thought of wanting; of vendors with an urgent "Who's next?" rushing people to buy ices and cotton candy and candied apples and sodas and sausage-and-pepper heros and other sweets and hots and greasies and frosties they weren't really hungry for. And always there was the sound of customers fussing for their money's worth. Like the woman too fat for her hot pants demanding a little more sugar on her zeppoles, and the boy, emboldened by his cronies, demanding the large pickle at the *bottom* of the jar from the "Candy Stand" man a few feet from Beryl.

When Randy finally reached her, Beryl grabbed her sister's hand and headed left for the Whip.

"Ma said no Whip," Randy chided, with a yank on Beryl's arm.

"She said no thing that flings you around in circles."

"And you know she meant the Whip, so don't even try it."

"I'm sure she meant those little whirlybird planes, and I promise I won't ask to go on that."

"Beryl!"

"Pretty please, Randy. Just let me go on it once. I'll give you a quarter."

"And if you get hurt I'll get in trouble."

"I won't get hurt. I promise. They strap you in real good. And if I do get hurt I'll tell them it was my fault and to give me the trouble when I get healed." Beryl put on her best pity-me face and turned up the whine. "Please-please, pretty please, Randy, just let me go on the Whip one little time."

"Okay," Randy gave in. "But just once. And remember, you owe me."

So Beryl had her way and a good scream as she got jerked and lurched and spun and twirled this way and that way, around and around. When the ride was over she stumbled down the ramp breathless, with her hair sticking up, and wild, glistening eyes. When she reached Randy she grabbed her hand, pitified her face, and pleaded, "Just one more time, Randy, just one more time . . . Pretty please?"

"No! You see, you see, you're never satisfied. Now if you ask me again we're going upstairs." Randy's voice was as strong as the grip she used to pull Beryl away.

"You're hurting me, and I'm gonna tell," Beryl whined as they moved away from the Whip. She tried to break free, but Randy's hand was tight-tight around her wrist, and she wasn't letting go. Beryl planted her feet flat on the ground and leaned *hard* away from Randy. It was tug-of-war, with Beryl's arm as the rope.

"Beryl, if you don't act right I'm gonna make you go upstairs!"

"If I have to go up, you will too!"

"Uh-uh. I'll be able to come back down, but you'll be upstairs only able to listen to everybody else having fun." With that, Randy got in a good yank.

Beryl stumbled forward a few steps, then she steadied herself, dug in her heels and reared her body back, flinging a defiant "You can't make me go upstairs" in Randy's face.

"Oh, yea-a-ah!" Randy threatened, right hand poised for a slap upside Beryl's head.

"Yea-a-ah," Beryl sneered. "And if you hit me I'm gonna tell," she shouted as she leaned herself hard to the right, and braced herself against Randy's inevitable tug forward. But instead of getting in another tug, Randy got mean. She let go, and Beryl flew back and to the ground.

"You made me fall," Beryl whined, on the verge of tears.

Then, from somewhere up above her head and over on the sidewalk, she heard, "You girls having a problem?"

"Daddy!" she screamed as she scrambled up and dashed over to her father.

"You giving Randy a hard time?" Mr. Nelson asked.

"Why you always think I'm the one making trouble, Daddy?" Beryl pouted as she threw her arms around her father and gave Randy a look that said, "I dare you to touch me now."

"Hi, Daddy," Randy said on her way to give him a quick kiss on the cheek.

"Beryl giving you trouble?" asked Mr. Nelson.

Now Beryl's eyes pleaded, Please don't tell on me.

"Not too much," Randy said, cutting her eyes at Beryl.

"Beryl, if you can't mind Randy you'll have to come on upstairs," Mr. Nelson warned.

"Daddy, you always take her side. You never ask if she's giving me any trouble, and believe me, Daddy, she—"

"Beryl . . ." Mr. Nelson said sternly. And that was all he needed to say, usually. That and maybe "You know better than that" or "I'm disappointed in you." It wasn't what he said, but that terrible tone his voice took on. Low, somber, or as Beryl put it, "rumbly."

"And why's your hair sticking up?" Mr. Nelson asked.

"I, uh, I . . . the wind did it."

"The wind?" Mr. Nelson glanced over his shoulder in the direction of the Whip.

How long had he been in the block? Beryl didn't dare ask.

"Yeah, Daddy, the wind," she said, thinking, well, that is the truth—in a way. "One of those big ole gusts."

"I see." Mr. Nelson made no other comment as he moved toward the building with a daughter on either side.

As they reached the steps, Beryl asked, "Daddy, you gonna be working overtime every night this week?"

"Looks that way."

"Then you won't get to spend any time at the carnival, right?"

"Looks that way."

"So you want us to come down here for you tomorrow and Thursday?"

"Beryl, didn't we say y'all could come down today, Wednesday, and Friday?"

"But I thought maybe we could come the other days for you and Ma. We could be your subs."

"How 'bout you just have fun for me and your mother on the nights we've already said yes to."

"But I only have enough money to have fun for myself," Beryl countered. "If I had, like, another dollar," she added with her sweet, baby-girl smile, "I could have a lot of fun for you tonight."

Mr. Nelson chuckled, reaching into his pants pocket. Beryl's hand went out for the dollar bill as it emerged.

"Fifty cents apiece," Mr. Nelson commanded, as he handed the dollar to Randy.

"How come she gets to hold it?" Beryl griped.

"Because she's the oldest, and she's in charge. 'Course, if you have a problem with that you can come on upstairs with me right now."

"No problem, Daddy, no problem," Beryl chirped.

" 'Bye, Daddy," said the sisters almost in unison, waving him into the building. As they headed back to the street and into the fair, they heard a "Hey, Beryl!" from somewhere in the crowd. Immediately Beryl recognized Linda's voice and craned her neck in search of her friend.

Linda Mays lived in one of the tenement buildings up the other side of the street. She was a light-brown, rather chubby girl with large and lovely eyes behind which lurked nothing but devilment and street-wise ways. That Linda was already wearing a training bra was only one point of envy for Beryl. Her friend's handball playing was another. As hard as she tried, Beryl could not yet get the low balls with her ease or flare. And what a champ Linda was when it came to standing up to the older kids who sometimes tried to bogart the court when she and Linda had next winners.

And Beryl envied Linda her mother, too. Miss Hazel worked nights at a club uptown and had men friends with Cadillacs and diamond pinky rings. Miss Hazel had lots of jewelry and false eyelashes like The Supremes. Miss Hazel wore a different hairstyle almost every day: long pony tail to the side one day, puffed up high the next, and down in a flip with bangs the day after that. To Beryl that was so amazing, even after Linda hipped her to the fact that it was all the work of wigs.

The best thing about Miss Hazel was all the stuff she let Linda do and have. Linda didn't have a real "be-upstairs-by" or "be-in-bed-by" time. The most her mother ever said about it as she left for work was, "Don't stay up too late." For Linda "too late" was sometimes eleven o'clock, sometimes midnight, and sometimes later than that—especially in the summer when she'd hang out on the stoop with some of the older girls in her building and learn how to cuss and how to make boys like her.

"Let's go win something," Linda suggested, flashing a five in Beryl's face.

Linda was never at a loss for money. Beryl had seen Miss Hazel give Linda one, two, three dollars one day, five the next, and ten on one super good-mood day. And in those days, when a twin pop cost a nickel, and a slice of pizza a quarter, ten dollars was a lot of money.

"Yeah! Let's go win something." Beryl was past ready. "Like what?"

"I don't know," Linda shrugged. "Something from over there."

She was pointing to a stall from the top of which hung a huge light blue teddy bear. When Linda turned and headed for it, Beryl followed.

"And where do you think you're going?" Randy called out.

"Just over there to win something," Beryl answered, sucking her teeth.

"Well, you can't because I want to go look for Rhonda."

"So can't you go look for her and let me meet you in front of the building in, like, fifteen minutes?"

"No. Ma said you have to stay with me, so you have to wait 'til I—"

"Hi, Randy."

It was Tyrone. Randy's voice switched quick from shrill to a purr. "Hi, Tyrone. How ya doin'?"

"Cool . . ." Tyrone shoved his hands in the back pockets of his jeans and took his man-of-the-world stance. "Wanna go get some ice cream?"

"Sure," Randy smiled. "That'd be nice."

Beryl didn't miss a beat. "Tell you what, Randy. You and Tyrone can go get some ice cream and then go look for Rhonda, and Linda and me will just be right over there, and I'll meet you in front of the building in like a half hour. How's that?" Beryl looked to Linda for some backup.

"And she won't be late because I got a watch," Linda smiled, thrusting her wrist up under Randy's nose so she could see it wasn't a toy watch.

Of course, Linda had a real watch. Linda had everything: a real leather jacket, Fred Braun shoes with taps, two pairs of Pro-Keds (a white pair, a black), an ID bracelet with her name in curlicues, a gold necklace with a heart-shaped charm clustered with (according to Linda) real diamonds, and matching earrings for her pierced ears. Beryl could live without a leather jacket, and a lot of the other stuff Linda had, but she'd give anything to have just one pair of Pro-Keds instead of her skips. She knew better than to hope for pierced ears anytime soon because her mother had said she wouldn't even consider it until she was thirteen. Randy would be fourteen soon and she was still wearing clip-ons.

"Okay, in a half hour," Randy said. As she and Tyrone headed for Mr. Softee, Beryl and Linda made their way over to the big blue bear.

Last year Beryl had lost fifteen nickels in her efforts to win a glass bowl from, she was sure, this very same grizzly-faced old man. It wasn't going to happen again, she swore, confident that because she was a little taller her reach would be better. This time her pitches would be on the money.

By the sixteenth pitch Beryl still hadn't won the candy dish she had her heart set on. As for Linda, she'd had fifty cents worth of bad luck with the ashtray she was aiming at. However, neither girl was ready to give up. Beryl's last pitch had clinked in and then skipped out of the candy dish and almost landed in a green bowl nearby. That was enough to keep hope alive. Plus, even though Beryl's pocket was running on empty, Linda still had enough dollars for more nickels than either of them could hold in one hand.

And so, the girls stood firm against the railing separating them from their would-be winnings. With elaborate leans and tiptoeing, and every kind of flick of the wrist they could think of, they continued to pitch nickel after nickel against the wind.

Until Randy arrived.

"Your time has long been up," she threatened as she stepped up behind Beryl, perfectly poised for a toss.

Beryl stamped her foot. "I was trying to concentrate!"

"It's almost 9:30. We gotta go."

"Just five more minutes," Beryl pleaded. "I know I'm gonna win, I just know it. I'm starting to feel lucky."

"Come on, Randy," Linda chimed in. "Just let her keep trying a little bit longer. And don't worry, when her money runs out I can give her another dollar."

"*Another* dollar!" Randy exploded. "How much have you lost already?"

"Not a lot," Beryl mumbled.

"Yeah, I bet. So you've spent up all your money and some of Linda's too?"

"But Randy, I want to win that candy dish for Ma and Daddy's anniversary present. You know how much Ma likes that crystal stuff."

"You know, you're really some kinda stupid!" Randy scolded. "First of all, it's not crystal; it's cheap glass. Second, you could've gone to Pepe's on Third Avenue and gotten *two* of those dishes with what you've already blown. Third," Randy added as she dragged Beryl away from the stall, "the surprise is gonna be enough of a present!"

3

The surprise was dinner for two at Chez Ours—as Randy had named the Nelson dinette for their parents' elegant anniversary dinner.

The backbone of the surprise was Grandma, who lived four floors above them. The sisters had imagined the evening, but it'd be Grandma who'd really make it happen. She had planned the menu: a salad of lettuces and endive, loin lamb chops, rice pilaf, sautéed cherry tomatoes and, at Beryl's nudging, string beans. "Make them the fancy kind," she had pleaded, meaning French-cut. When Randy had the bright idea of having cocktails before dinner and put her bid in for hors d'oeuvres—"like you make for those rich white people's parties"—Grandma promised an assortment of delectables, frilly toothpicks and all.

The only battleground was dessert. Grandma expounded on how well fruit compote or even sherbet with lace cookies would complement the meal, while the girls begged for her trademark peach cobbler.

"That's a cold weather dessert," Grandma explained. "Too heavy for this meal anyway." But the girls persisted, and in the end Grandma compromised. "I'll make a thin-crust berry cobbler. How's that?" A lukewarm "Okay" was how they responded, because they knew this was a final offer.

Grandma's help didn't come cheap, and it didn't come easy. Beryl and Randy had to chip in for the food as well as pitch in with the preparation.

"Learn how to do, or be a bum," Grandma would always say whenever they tried to lazy out of doing something that needed to be done with a whimpy-whiny "But I don't know how."

"Then you'll just have to learn," Grandma would declare.

And so, on that Friday evening before the surprise, instead of being at the carnival, the girls were at Grandma's—washing, slicing, chopping, dicing, measuring, mixing, and doing a ton of other little tasks that needed to be done to make a "fancy" dinner.

Before Beryl and Randy headed downstairs they rehearsed their game plan. Grandma quizzed them on everything from how to set the table to how to plate the food. For what seemed the hundredth time, she repeated instructions for the last-minute heating up and cooking Randy would have to do. Handing Randy a set of keys to her apartment, she said, "Remember: most everything'll be on the bottom shelf of the Frigidaire, and what-all don't need refrigerating will be on the stove. The breadbasket, candles, and serving things I'll leave on the counter by the sink. Got it?"

The next day everything went as planned. The morning was taken up with the Nelson Saturday morning ritual of breakfast and chores. Mr. and Mrs. Nelson pretended not to notice that the girls were particularly giggly and getting along a little too well.

When noon came, so did Grandma, ready to be taken on her errands. She warned her daughter and son-in-law that she'd probably have them running around with her until evening. With a wink to the girls, she said, "I know this means y'all will have to stay in the house all day, but I trust you'll be able to find something constructive to do."

"Don't worry, Grandma, we'll be fine," Beryl winked back. As her parents moved through the door, she heard her mother marvel, "Sure ain't like Beryl to not have a fit when she can't go outside."

With the apartment all to themselves now, Beryl and Randy got feverishly busy on the surprise, with bouts of bickering almost every other step of the way. Randy fussed at Beryl for not getting all the tarnish off the silverware. Beryl laughed at Randy when she got crinkles in the linen. Randy sent Beryl into a pout when she refused to let her wash the crystal glasses.

"I'll be *real* careful," Beryl promised.

"Like you were with Ma's good vase last Christmas?"

So it went from the time they began their work until late in the afternoon when they went up to Grandma's to tote down the food. By 4:45 all was well and ready at Chez Ours, and the girls were putting on their "uniforms": black skirts, white blouses, and floppy bow ties Randy fashioned from Mrs. Nelson's scarves. As the clock ticked close up on six, they were sitting anxiously in the living room waiting for the phone to ring. Soon, it did.

One . . . two . . . three? On the fourth ring they bolted to the kitchen. Randy's skittish "Hello" was met with Grandma's chipper, "They're on their way down!"

"But you were supposed to just ring twice and hang up," Randy said.

"I know, but I wanted to remind you not to overcook my lamb chops. Remember: three minutes on each side. I know your daddy likes his meat well done, but he'll just have to be happy with medium-rare tonight."

"Yes, Grandma," Randy responded. "Bye-bye."

"Bye, Grandma," Beryl yelled into the phone, only to be shushed by Randy and shooed away with "The chain. Go put the chain on."

Randy cut off all the lights on her way to the entrance

hall where she found Beryl with her ear pressed against the door. "Here," she whispered, tossing Beryl a white serving napkin.

Without removing her ear from the door, Beryl draped the napkin over her arm. "I hear the elevator. It's them. It's them!"

"Ssh!" Randy sprinted back down the hall and into the living room to take her place by the record player.

Yes, it was them all right. Beryl knew her parents' footsteps, but still she kept her ear hard against the door—as she heard the two sets of footsteps stop in front of the door, as she heard the rustling of packages and the jingle of her father's keys, as she heard—

"Ow!" is what her parents heard when Mr. Nelson opened the door.

"Just a minute!" Beryl rubbed her temple with one hand and with the other pushed the door closed and turned the lock. "Stay right there, don't move." She dashed midway down the hall and whisper-shouted, "Ready?"

At the sound of Randy's "Ready," Beryl rushed back to the front door, took a deep breath, unloosed the chain lock, and opened the door. With an elaborate bow and a flutter of her eyes, she greeted her parents with a loud, "Good evening, Monsieur and Madame. Welcome to Chez Ours!"

On cue, Randy let the arm down on the record, and Mr. and Mrs. Nelson heard Ben E. King drifting into:

There is a rose in Spanish Harlem . . .

The Nelson record collection was mostly gospel choirs and crusading quartets. But every once in awhile they allowed themselves some rhythm and blues.

"What in the world . . . ?" Mrs. Nelson beamed, but Beryl cut her mother off with "This way, please," and, full of pomp, ushered her parents down the hall and into the "lounge"—the far corner of the living room where the girls had set up a white-clothed card table and two folding chairs. The table was laid with a bowl of mixed nuts and an Eiffel-tower vase with a plastic red rose.

As they took it all in, the most Mr. and Mrs. Nelson could manage were sighs and chuckles of delight, and a few phrases like "Oh, my Lord!" and "What is this?" and "Well, I'll be!" Mrs. Nelson let out a gasp of cautious joy when she looked across the room and saw that the archway into the dinette was now a wall of pink crepe paper.

"Please be seated," Beryl commanded. As she spun away, Randy came forward with a platter of hors d'oeuvres and two stemmed glasses. A few seconds later Beryl returned with a bottle of grape juice in one hand and a bottle of ginger ale in the other. With a mischievous gleam in her eye, she asked, "Red wine or white?"

Having served her father "white" and her mother "red," Beryl headed back to the kitchen to help Randy with the final fixings. Before she slipped behind the curtain, she said, "Now stay right here. You can't leave the lounge until we say so." For once the shoe was on the other foot; she was doing the bossing, her parents, the obeying.

From all the opening and closing of the kitchen cabinets, the broiler, oven, and refrigerator doors, from all the pings, clings, clangs, and rattle of dishes, silver, and glass, Mr. and Mrs. Nelson knew their daughters were up to something extra special. And from the aromas that drifted into the "lounge," it smelled like quite a delicious something special. Bursting with excitement and a childlike wonder, they almost leapt from their seats when Beryl poked her head through the crepe paper curtain and issued what would be her last command of the night. "Okay, y'all can leave the lounge now. Dinner is served."

Beryl and Randy stood at attention on either side of the curtain. When their parents reached them, the girls flung the curtain back and exclaimed,

"Happy Anniversary!"

"Oh, my goodness!" Mrs. Nelson's eyes darted around the table so properly set with her "good" dishes, her crystal glasses, her wedding silverware. She suppressed a chuckle at the sight of her two squat cut-glass candleholders into which the girls had planted too-tall red candles. She marveled "Oh, how precious!" at the bevy of pink origami swans at the center of the table.

"I made these," Beryl announced, pointing to the three that looked more like sick pterodactyls than swans. "And aren't they magnificent?" her mother smiled.

"Looka there, looka there," was all Mr. Nelson could say as he gave the food the once-over. Like his wife, he was at a serious loss for words; and he, too, smothered the girls with hugs and kisses. Beryl saw tears glistening in her mother's eyes and for a split second she thought she caught a little sparkle in her father's.

"Are you really surprised?" Beryl was jittering between her parents, looking from one to the other.

"You sure got us this time," Mrs. Nelson replied.

Beryl couldn't remember a last time, but okay, she thought. "You mean it?" she pressed her mother. "Daddy, y'all really had no idea?"

"No, popcorn, not a clue."

"So we really surprised you?"

Mrs. Nelson cupped Beryl's face in her hand and gave it a baby shake. "Yes, sweetheart, you really surprised us."

"Prove it. I mean— You know what I mean. Were you really, really, really, *really* surprised?"

"Yes, Beryl, they were," Randy said as she marched her by the shoulders into the kitchen. "But if you don't stop pestering them they won't really, really, really, *really* get to enjoy it."

———

The girls had planned to eat in their room while their parents had their private dinner for two, but Mr. and Mrs. Nelson wouldn't have it. As they all dined together they heaped praises on the girls, and in the process gave themselves a little pat on the back. They'd both come from no-collar folk and were very proud of the progress they had made that let them do better for their daughters.

There were times when Mr. Nelson hardly saw his daughters until the weekend, because they were fast asleep when he left for work and when he returned. When Beryl or Randy complained, "Why you *always* working?" he'd respond, "So you can have all of what you need, and some of what you want."

Mrs. Nelson was always working, too, only at home. Her neighbor Sadie used to badger her about getting an outside job. "Daniel don't want you to work so's he can keep his foot on your neck. He knows if you had your own money you'd be doing as you pleased." But Mrs. Nelson had no problem doing as she and her husband had agreed.

After working two and, some seasons, three jobs early on in their marriage, Mr. Nelson was down to one at the coat company where he was a shipping manager. But many days he still left early and came home late, making that overtime money.

Mrs. Nelson worked at stretching his paycheck so there'd be all that much more to save. She bought more fresh than canned or frozen, and made from scratch instead of from quick-mix, and mended to keep from replacing. And she was there for Randy and Beryl: to help with homework, to monitor chores, to just be there so they'd know they couldn't stray too far on their way home.

Mr. and Mrs. Nelson attributed their progress in life to their own hard work, but ultimately to the grace of God. With rare exception they attended church every Sunday and did their fair share of church work as well. And they saw raising their daughters as their number one duty. Beryl and Randy were souls God had entrusted them with, to keep and train up in the way that they should go. As Mr. and Mrs. Nelson basked in the warmth of Beryl and Randy's surprise, they dared to think maybe they were doing it right.

Mrs. Nelson rose to make a toast. "To my lovely daughters who never cease to amaze me." She paused to blink back the tears. "Thank you very, very much. You'll never know how proud you've made us this night."

As the family clinked glasses, Mr. Nelson followed up with, "Girls, you've really outdone yourselves. It's moments like this that make me appreciate all the more how very blessed I am to have you two as my daughters." The family touched glasses again, and Mr. and Mrs. Nelson sat down.

"I got a toast!" Beryl shot up. She really didn't, but

she wasn't going to let that stop her. "To the best parents in the world . . . We love you, and we, uh . . . Congratulations on your— How long you been married?"

"Twelve wonderful years," Mrs. Nelson responded, with a tender glance at her husband.

"And so," Beryl resumed her toast, "Congratulations on your—"

She broke off because of some squirming in her mind. "But that can't be," she frowned. "Randy is thirteen, so—" After a split-second pause, she gasped, "You mean, y'all had Randy *before* you were married?"

During the very long pause, Mrs. Nelson shifted in her chair. Randy dropped her head, and Mr. Nelson was looking puzzled. "You never told her?" he asked. It was more an accusation than a question.

"Told me what?!" Beryl demanded, frantically searching her parents' eyes. In her father's she found annoyance, in her mother's, embarrassment. When she looked across the table at Randy she saw . . . no shock, no surprise, no curiosity. No nothing. Randy just sat there, expressionless.

"Well," Beryl stammered, "I guess it's okay and everything . . . because you ended up getting married."

Beryl saw how stern her father's face was now fixed, and when he turned to her and cleared his throat, she had a feeling that something terrible was about to come out of his mouth.

"Beryl, when I met your mother Randy was six

months old. I came to love them both very, very much. So when your mother and me decided to get married, it was only right and natural that I'd become Randy's father and raise her up as my own child." After a pause, he added, "I thought your mother had told you all about this by now."

Beryl waited for what else he had to say, because what she'd just heard made absolutely no sense. What was he talking about? How could Randy be born before her parents even met— "You mean . . . you're not Randy's . . . *real* daddy?"

"No. I'm not her natural father."

Beryl looked at her mother, then back at her father, then back at her mother. Her voice almost a whisper, she asked, "So, Mommy . . . you were married one time before?"

"Well, no, Beryl, I wasn't." Mrs. Nelson's reply was so solemn. "I know this is probably a little confusing for you but, um . . . I, you see, uh . . . ."

Beryl had never seen her mother hem and haw so. It terrified her. "You *what*?" she shrieked.

As the moments of stone-silence piled up, bits and pieces of hushed conversations and strange silences flashed into remembrance. Like the time she heard her mother on the phone with a long-ago friend sigh, "Daniel is the best thing that ever happened to me and Randy." Like the time Miss Sadie was flipping through their photo album and squawked, "Beryl sure looks like

Daniel spit her out . . . but Randy don't look like she belongs to either of you."

Beryl's remembering came to an abrupt end when her mother broke into her thoughts with: "I tell you what . . . why don't we just get back to this wonderful dinner, and we'll talk about this later."

Beryl didn't want to talk about it *later*. She wanted to talk about it Now! But her parents gave her a chastising look that said, "No, *not* now."

Too trembly inside to protest, she bolted from the dinner table and down the hall to her bedroom. Once inside, she headed for her bed, then pivoted back to the door. She slammed it shut with all her might.

"Beryl! Get back in here this minute!" Mr. Nelson thundered from the dinette.

"Daniel, I'll handle it," Beryl heard faintly through her closed door.

She listened intently for footsteps so she'd know which pose to strike. Had she heard heavy, slow steps, she would have flung herself onto her bed and let her tears flow. But the footsteps were light, and so she plopped down on her bed with her back to the door, arms crossed over her chest, mouth in full pout.

"Oh, baby," Mrs. Nelson cooed as she entered the room. "There, there," she sighed as she sat down beside her. Cuddling Beryl up into her arms, she added, "Lord knows this ain't nothing to be getting so upset about."

At that Beryl burst into tears that mounted to wrenching sobs so loud that they drowned out the heavy, slow footsteps coming down the hall.

"What in the world's got a-holt of you?!" Mr. Nelson boomed from the doorway. Beryl stopped crying mid-sob. Then, with sniffles and a furrowed brow, she whined, "It's just that, that nobody ever told me, and it's so horrible and nobody said sorry, and—"

"Horrible?" Mr. Nelson scowled. "What's so horrible and what's anybody got to be sorry for?"

"For not telling me, for keeping secrets from me, for . . ." Beryl trailed off into more tears and sniffle spasms. She had no words for her confusion, her sorrow, her anger. She listened hungrily for words of relief as her parents took turns trying to straighten her out, settle her down. Mr. Nelson gave her the bare facts of the matter surrounding Randy's adoption, while Mrs. Nelson served up platitudes and vague answers to Beryl's barrage of questions.

The most frightening discovery was that Randy's father was alive. Most vexing of all was that it was her mother's fault that she'd been kept in the dark about the matter. "I was waiting for the right time," Mrs. Nelson offered by way of comfort. " 'Til you were a little older."

Older? Beryl wondered. I'll be eleven soon. Then, oh no! she thought before she asked out loud, "Daddy, are you *my* real daddy?"

"Yes, I am."

"You swear?"

"Yes, Beryl, I swear."

She looked at him hard, and then down at her arms, her legs, seeing as if for the first time that she was almost as dark as her father. She glanced in the mirror above the vanity to double-check that she really did look as much like him as people often said. Her mouth was like his, not small and thin-lipped like her mother's, and she had his large ears, and his wide eyes.

Beryl felt somewhat steadier after this, and ready with more questions.

But Mr. Nelson brought the conversation to a close with, "Look, Beryl, you know the truth now and, as we know, the truth shall set you free. So go free your face from those tearstains and get on back to the table for dessert. After all, when all is said and done, nothing's different. What matters is that we're family now."

Beryl obediently went to the bathroom, washed her face, and returned to Chez Ours for dessert, but she refused to believe that nothing was different. Things *had* changed.

She looked at her mother and thought about all the times she'd told her that honesty was the best policy. And yet, it had been her mother who had kept the truth from her. And didn't her mother number among those grown-ups who preached that "nice girls" don't have s-e-x until they marry? And yet . . . As Beryl dwelled on these contradictions she came to the conclusion that her mother was not an honest woman and had not been a nice girl.

And what did this make her father? She wasn't quite sure yet. And maybe she was wrong when all along she'd been thinking he loved Randy the best.

And Randy? She was just a half-sister. Half-sister? The word left her feeling lonely and scared, and with a head full of "what-ifs."

Beryl only nibbled at her dessert. She did not taste the sweetness of the berries, and the crust could have been cardboard or sawdust or air. With each bite she thought she'd choke on the silence at Chez Ours.

4

It wasn't a dark and stormy night, but such would have fit Beryl's mood quite well. A little thunder, and some lightning, mingled with eerie whistles of a faraway wind would have greatly helped with the brooding. But, no. Beryl's mind was left to tussle and churn against a luscious night, with a gauzy moon and a toss of stars you'd never name "Twinkle," but maybe "Tickle." Or "Kiss-Me-Sweet," perhaps. And the sudden waves of breeze had the cool and charm of a seaside scene.

Bathed and dusted with honeysuckle talc, Beryl lay in bed only half-hearing a fire engine sirening in the distance, and the racket and loose laughter from the carnival.

"How long you known?" Though Randy was stone-still and flat on her back, Beryl knew she was not yet asleep. She heard Randy's annoyance in her sigh.

"Since I was a little kid."

39

"Who told you?"

"Daddy."

"You mean *my* daddy?"

"Yeah, Beryl . . . *your* daddy."

"I didn't mean it that way," Beryl insisted.

But didn't she?

Randy reached back to that hazy-hot day at Coney Island. All four of them were there, she knew, but in her remembering she could never see her mother and "Berry," as she used to say her sister's name. She only saw Mr. Nelson handing her a gigantic spin of rainbow cotton candy. And then . . .

And then, they were walking, just the two of them. On the boardwalk. She'd be going to school soon, for the first time. "I'll always be your daddy and you'll always be my daughter," he was saying, and then something about another father. "Will he buy cotton candy for me?" was the only question she had then.

But as she grew older she had more. She had tried to piece together the how and why of it all, with very little help from Mrs. Nelson. For the missing pieces, Randy worked in assumptions. Mr. Nelson never seemed bothered by her questions, but his answers were so plain. Like the time she asked why he had to tell her in the first place. "You were bound to find out someday" was his reply. "Didn't want you to hear it from somebody else." And in his tone she heard, "See, it's that simple." But it wasn't that simple for Randy. And now Beryl, with her questions, was making her think about all the questions she'd gotten in the habit of being afraid to ask.

"You ever met him?" Beryl asked.

"Ma says so. When I was real little. But I don't remember."

"Where's he at now?"

"I dunno."

"Don't you want to know?"

"No. Not really. And I don't feel like playing twenty questions, either."

"I thought maybe . . . Aren't you curious? Do you ever sort of miss him, or something?"

"How I'm gonna miss somebody I don't know?"

"Could be he might find out where we live and then come for you one day and tell Daddy he can't be your daddy no more, and say you have to go live with him. Would you leave us?"

"That's a stupid question."

"What if he's rich?"

The carnival was winding down for the night. What music there was, was blocks away, and with the crowd thinning, the sounds of individual lives were becoming more and more distinct. Beryl heard Mrs. Richardson on the second floor yell out the window for Stella to "get upstairs right this minute!" From farther down, on the walkway behind her building, she heard a woman's mousy "Tony, staahhp. You said you just wanted to talk to me." Beryl imagined the woman flipping her hair, heavy with hair spray, behind her shoulder. From Tony's "Eh, Angie . . ." she imagined him one of the white-shoed Eye-talians in Randy's poem. Then came the sound of talk from her parents' bedroom.

She couldn't make out the words, only voices stepping on each other. But her father wasn't sounding rumbly, and her mother wasn't fast and fussy, and Beryl's stomach didn't have that jumpy, icky-sicky feeling that told her they were arguing, no matter how low they talked or how hard they tried to pretend they weren't when she and Randy were around. So, no, they weren't fighting.

Beryl heard something drop on the floor. Then she heard the closet door sliding, then sliding again, with a knock at the wall, which meant the last slide was its closing. And now, her mother was talking. From the way her voice tipped up at the end, she was asking questions. Then her voice flattened out.

Beryl was about to get out of bed and tip to the wall that separated their bedrooms, hoping to catch enough words to at least know if they were talking about it, talking about her—when her mother stopped talking.

Beryl waited for her father's voice to step in.

Beryl waited for her mother's to start up again.

Beryl listened for an end to the silence, but it never came. Not after five minutes. Not after ten minutes.

"Randy? . . . Randy?"

"What is it *now*?"

"Don't you even want to know what he looks like?"

"I do know."

"How?" Beryl sat bolt upright.

"I got a picture."

"Can I see it?"

"No."

"Why not?" Beryl whined. "That's not fair."

"And neither is your hair." There was anger in Randy's tease.

"Oh, come on. *Please.*"

"No! Now leave me alone."

It was as if Randy had slammed a door in her face, and as Randy turned onto her side with her back to her sister, Beryl lay down and swallowed the rest of her questions.

5

Sunday morning meant salmon croquettes and scrambled eggs and grits, and getting dressed up for God.

Very starched, frilly-girly dresses that sometimes scratched, and crinolines and lacy-like socks and patent leather shoes, and panties with ruffles and that thin elastic that left a little dent in her waist were so . . . so always that Beryl never thought to ask what would happen if she went to church on a Sunday in her playclothes or a school outfit.

Besides, she wanted God to like her, and if Sunday Best helped, okay. Maybe it would help keep God from staying mad at her. Since He was forever "watchin' " as Pastor Stone was always so scarily saying, she knew God probably stayed mad at her for long times.

Grandma had told her that the Almighty didn't go around staying mad at people. She had said that, yes, God was indeed "watchin' " but not for a reason to frown down, but because "He's longing to love you." Whenever Grandma talked about God, Beryl didn't get scared, but felt like liking God a lot. The only thing she couldn't understand was if Grandma liked God so much why she didn't go to church with them more often. And the only thing she ever wondered about Sunday Best was if God knew that some Sundays she'd sneak off her fancy panties and put on a pair of her everyday ones, which didn't pinch her waist.

Beryl had once asked her mother if God could see through your clothes. "Don't be fresh," Mrs. Nelson had replied. It was the same response she'd gotten when she'd asked, "How come we don't say grace when we're out in the parking lot at Dairy Queen with our chili dogs and slushies?"

Now, as she sat in the kitchen in her underclothes and a towel around her shoulders and a telephone book highchairing her almost level with the stove, she figured her mother would say this very same thing if she asked if God had gotten mad at her when she had a baby without having a husband.

Mrs. Nelson was hum-singing "Rock of Ages" as she ran a warm straightening comb through Beryl's hair. Randy was old enough for a hard press and the privilege of doing her own hair, with trips to Miss Lucille's for a press and curl for special occasions. But for Beryl it was still that yellow-green stuff, which smelled like rotten eggs, that Mrs. Nelson applied every few months to make her hair "more manageable" for twisted pufftails like she was getting today.

"Ma, you gonna let Randy get a Afro like Rhonda?"

"Not as long as I'm clothed in my right mind."

"She wants one real bad, you know."

"I know. And she can have one—"

"But you just said—"

"When she's grown and out on her own, by which time I sincerely hope this wildness will be out of style."

"But, Ma, Rhonda don't look so bad with her Afro. Like a dandelion after it's had its yellow head."

"But Rhonda ain't my child."

"Ruthie Mae," Mr. Nelson was calling out as he made his way into the kitchen, tucking his shirt into his trousers. "Honey, where's that tie clip Aunt Bert gave me last year?"

"On the dresser where I told you I was putting it last night when I laid out your suit and shirt and tie, Daniel Obadiah Nelson," answered Mrs. Nelson with a look that said, Sometimes I don't know where your mind is but I love you anyway, and forever.

Her parents had that smoochy-smoochy tone of voice, which made Beryl want to wag her finger "ooooh" and giggle up at the same time.

"Ruthie Mae, Ruthie Mae. What would I do without you?" Mr. Nelson smiled as he made his exit. He returned a few minutes later, fully dressed. With arms

46

outstretched, he asked, "How do I look, Ruthie Mae? Did I get it right?"

"Go'n, Daniel Obadiah," Mrs. Nelson waved him away.

Beryl knew Sunday was the Lord's day, but she hoped He didn't mind sharing it with her daddy. On him Sunday Best looked so right and natural, and it didn't seem as if anything was pinching. She wished he could wear his black or navy blue suit and a white shirt and a dress-up tie every day of the week. He always looked so tall.

"Am I ever gonna get a little sister or brother?"

"Anything's possible, popcorn," Mr. Nelson replied. With a glance and a grin at his wife, he added, "And I'm always ready to explore the possibilities."

"Daniel, behave yourself," tsked Mrs. Nelson, and Beryl could tell she was smiling.

"Just want to make sure you know that, Ruthie Mae."

"Believe me, honey, I do."

Beryl was dead-serious about her question and here her parents were doing smoochy-smoochy talk. "Come on, you guys," she whined. "I want y'all to have a baby."

"And why-so, popcorn?"

"So I can have a real sister."

"That's enough, Beryl," said Mrs. Nelson, and Beryl knew she definitely was not smiling.

When they arrived at church Mr. Nelson headed for his preferred pew. Randy and Beryl sat on either side.

Mrs. Nelson was soon on her post a few rows behind them.

Beryl always liked it when her mother's group was serving as ushers. Sure, she could sometimes feel her mother's eyes on the back of her head, but from where she stood her mother couldn't see *everything*. She couldn't help people get seated, pass out fans *and* watch Beryl's every move, too. Her father didn't check every other minute to make sure she was sitting up straight. When she yawned, he never glared at her like, Have you forgotten where you are?

During most of the service Beryl did in fact forget where she was and why she was there. There were moments when she truly did want to understand what everybody was singing and praying about, but it was hard to keep her mind from wandering.

Like to the fans, and how all the old, old people did it slow and easy, but others did it so fast. Her mother had said fast fanning only made you hotter.

Like to the choir, and why most everybody up there looked like they were on punishment. And poor Brother Poole. He sure did sweat, and since he couldn't very well wipe his face while he was singing he had to just drip, drip, drip until the song was over. Swimming Poole, and a singing fool, Beryl singsonged in her head.

And like to the hats, the hats, the so many hats. Round and square, and some like a pirate's, and most of them with feathers or fruits or flowers and some with a little of all, and maybe some beads, or a patent leather bow. Yellow, pink, blue, black, purple, gold, white, green, lavender, orange, and other colors Beryl didn't know how to call. The ladies in her church had prettier hats than the movie stars. And she was holding a hat contest, casting her vote for the number 1, 2 and 3 she'd wear if she were a grown lady.

At sermon time Beryl came back to where she was, ready to pay attention, so when her parents later asked, "And what did you learn today?" she'd have an answer, though she'd recently figured out that "Jesus loves me" always worked.

Right now, it was impossible not to pay attention, what with that strange silence. It was as if a troop of angels charged through the doors of the sanctuary and announced, "All right, everybody, shut up, now! God is on the way in." And then Pastor Stone stepped up to the pulpit and looked out over the congregation in a way that always made Beryl want to ask, "What'd *I* do?"

"I am going to speak today," intoned Pastor Stone, "from the book of Proverbs, chapter 11, verse 13."

Beryl dawdled over the word Proverbs, seeing it in the heavy lettering in the big Bible at home. Wonder if there's a book of Pronouns? Pastor Stone was already into his recitation of the scripture when another word caught her attention: Secrets. When he paused, Beryl waited intently for him to repeat the verse, which he always did.

"A talebearer revealeth secrets; but he that is of a faithful spirit concealeth the matter."

Beryl glanced over her shoulder at her mother. Mrs. Nelson glared at her to face front.

Is this why she kept it from me? Beryl wondered. She wasn't sure what talebearer meant, but the way Pastor Stone hit the word, she figured it was a very bad thing to be. Must be like tattletale, only much, much worse. And telling a tale meant telling a lie. But the thing about Randy wasn't a lie, so her mother wasn't being a "faithful spirit" in keeping it from her.

Weird and squeezy her head was feeling. Is this what grownups feel when they have a headache? Beryl didn't want to listen to anything, anymore. She leaned her head against her father's shoulder.

"I'd planned to speak on something else, today, but it's come to my attention that some of you folks have been having a *TIME* with your tongues lately. Talking other people's business, spreading confusion. And as James taught us, 'For every kind of beasts, and of birds, and of serpents, and of things in the sea, is tamed, and hath been tamed of mankind: But the tongue can no man tame; it is an unruly evil, full of deadly poison.' Poison kills, church. Poison *kills*! Church, you better watch your tongue!"

Beryl could swear Pastor Stone was looking straight at her.

"And I'm here to tell you, today, that the Almighty

hates gossips more than he hates fools, and whore-mongers, and liars, and thieves. I'm here to warn you, today, that if someone tells you something in confidence, you best keep that secret if you want to be right with God."

There was a sprinkling of half-hearted "Amens." One lone lady yelled out, "Tell it, Pastor, tell it!" That was Sister Cox. Beryl remembered overhearing Miss Sadie telling her mother the other day, "Well, I heard" something, something, something about Sister Cox's son.

The congregation was still, tight. The air had a strange heat. A lot of people were fast-fanning. Old folks, too. It always got this way when Pastor Stone did what he called his "duty" as "Chastiser," which to Beryl he seemed to do a whole lot of the time. She felt sorry for his kids.

As he continued on with his sermon, the sound of his voice and the whop of the fans dimmed, and after a few bobs to the left, to the right, Beryl's head listed long to the right and into the resting place of her father's arm. It seemed only a moment later that he was patting her leg. When she opened her eyes Pastor Stone was seated in his chair, looking very puffed up and pleased with himself. The choir was on its feet and Brother Poole was swaying into a solemn song. It was just him and the choir until Pastor Stone rose, motioning for the congregation to sing along. They pitched in only for the refrain: "Please be patient with me, God's not through with me yet."

6

Mr. and Mrs. Nelson tried to keep their Sabbath close to what they understood it was supposed to be: A day of rest. In the morning they rested their souls in the sanctuary, and in the afternoon and evening, their minds and bodies, and almost always at home. There'd be an early full dinner, often courtesy of Grandma, who joined them only if she really felt like it.

After dinner the girls were pretty much free to do as they pleased only they couldn't go very far. Not outside, not to a friend's house, and not into too much TV. Unless the afternoon movie starred Jerry Lewis or Godzilla, there usually wasn't too much they wanted to see until early evening when "Wild Kingdom" came on, with old Marlin Perkins doing all the talking and his younger sidekick doing all the dangerous stuff with the animals. At eight o'clock came "The Ed Sullivan Show" where they occasionally got to see The Supremes or some other black people being fabulous and famous.

The sisters spent some Sunday afternoons playing Old Maid, or War, or a board game like Life or Sorry. But this was only when Randy wasn't acting grown, holed up on her bed as if it were an island in the middle of a vast nowhere. She'd read. Or write. Or make lanyard somethings for her friends, key chains mostly. These days she worked the alligator stitch, long bored with the box stitch, which Beryl was just getting good at.

Randy had her grown self out this Sunday, along with a small spiral notebook. Beryl figured she was making poetry.

"Can I see what you writing?" Beryl had asked at one point, more out of boredom with herself than anything else. Randy hadn't even looked up for her curt "No." So Beryl had gone back to her game of Pick-Up Sticks, which had come after Cherries-In-A-Basket, Firecrackers, and a few other varieties of jacks. When she grew tired of Pick-Up Sticks, she took up her bat-and-ball.

Pap, pap, pap, pap, pap, pap,— Pap, pap—Pap, pap, pap, pap— Pap, pap, pap, pap, pap, pap, pap, pap, pap, pap, pap, pap—

"Will you stop that!" Randy snapped. "Can't you see I'm trying to concentrate?"

"Dag! You act like you own this room." Beryl had an urge to keep pap, pap, papping as long and as hard as she could. But she changed her mind, because maybe if she didn't get on Randy's nerves too bad she'd let her see what she was writing in a little while, or maybe she'd be making some lanyard things tonight. Randy had promised to teach her the alligator stitch soon. So Beryl took up a less noisy something: her drawing tablet and her deluxe box of Crayolas, with the sharpener on the back.

"Randy," Mrs. Nelson called on her way down the hall. "Grandma's got your outfits for the trip all but ready, and wants you to come up for a final fit." To Randy's heavy sigh and a slight teeth-suck, she replied, "What's that?"

"Nothing."

"Well, I suggest you change the tone of that nothing of yours," Mrs. Nelson warned on her way back up the hall.

"Can I go try on what she made me now?" Beryl asked.

"No, she's not finished with your things yet."

Randy slouched up from her bed and into her flip-flaps. Her notebook disappeared under her bed. As she flip-flapped by, Beryl snickered, "Guess she didn't know you were concentrating."

"Shut up, shrimp!"

"Make me," Beryl said, with a little strut of her neck.

"You little . . ." Randy's stare was cold, and killing. She was a high-up-in-the-sky hawk, Beryl a wounded rabbit. Then, as if this helpless creature wasn't worth the effort, Randy haughtily moved on.

Didn't stare me down that time, Beryl humphed. Her victory was sweet but short. Randy pivoted back and kicked Beryl's Crayolas hard. She stepped lively from the room with a sinister giggle.

"Creep!" Beryl shouted.

"Takes one to know one," Randy shouted back from the entrance hall.

"Y'all having a problem in there?" Mr. Nelson called out from the living room.

Randy's voice was sugary sweet. "No, just kidding around," she said, and the next thing Beryl heard was the front door close.

She felt a cry coming on. Randy always got "last tag." "I'll fix her," Beryl hissed, as wicked thoughts quelled the tears.

She was thinking of jumbling everything up in Randy's chest of drawers, or hiding her earrings, or putting something nasty in her hairbrush. But then, as she belly-crawled under her bed to retrieve a scattering of crayons, she caught sight of an even better idea.

Through the bedspread's skinny fringe she was eyeing Randy's keepsake box, where she kept that little spiral notebook, and what-all else Beryl didn't know. "Bet that's where she keeps his picture," she whispered.

Beryl made her way over to Randy's bed and slid out the black-lacquered box flecked with small peacocks and gemstones. It had a gold-toned lock shaped like a diamond, as were the two hinges on the back. It had been a gift to Grandma from one of the ladies she worked for, something the woman had brought back for "her Essie" from a trip to the Orient. Grandma had thought it nice enough, while for Randy it was love at first sight and she hadn't had to beg too hard before it was hers.

"Shh . . . *oot!*" It was locked. Of course, it was.

Beryl sprang up and went for a hairpin from the dresser set on the vanity. It worked in spy movies. When it didn't work for her, she threw the hairpin on the floor and began to search for the key. Where would Randy keep it?

In the drawer of the nightstand? In her jewelry box? In her underwear drawer? Under her pillow? What had Randy done after she got up from the bed and before she got to me? Beryl strained to remember. "Think, stupid, think," she muttered. "She bent over and reached under her bed and then . . . and then . . . Shh . . . *oot!*"

Beryl stamped her foot in defeat, having recalled that there had been jingling every step of the way—when Randy reached under the bed, when she walked across the room, when she said, "Shut up, shrimp," when she flip-flapped from the room. Ever since Randy had gotten her own set of keys last year, she never left the house without them. And where else would she keep the little key to her keepsake box?

Beryl glared at the box for a hot minute, first tempted to kick it, then to try out her powers of concentration like The Amazing Babini whom she'd once seen pop a lock with his bare eyes on "The Ed Sullivan Show." She squatted down to shove the box back under the bed. At the touch of a hinge she whispered, "Hey, wait a minute." She turned the box around for a good look at the back. "Uh-huh, they don't look so strong," she smiled.

Beryl crept from the room and to the skinny catchall closet in the entrance hall. Without a sound, she eased a screwdriver out of the old paint can in which her father kept his most-used tools. The closet door creaked on the close, and she froze.

Silence.

She hadn't been heard. She could breathe again. But why take chances? She left the closet door ajar. With the screwdriver behind her back, she tipped to her room, easing that door to a quiet close.

The hinges of the keepsake box popped off, no sweat, and pingled to the floor. "Gotcha!" Beryl rejoiced.

And what treasures she found. A lipstick, an eyebrow pencil, and the little spiral notebook, of course. And letters from the pen pal in Holland that Randy had until Rhonda questioned, "What you got to talk about with some girl who wears ugly clogs and plants tulips?" There was Randy's autograph book from elementary school with partings like: "We'll never say good-bye. Only see you later. Your friend forever, Sharon." Sharon? Beryl puzzled. Randy don't have no friend named Sharon.

There were photos of Randy with Rhonda and some other girls whose names Beryl couldn't remember, and a few with Randy's used-to-be best friend, Vickie, who moved to the Bronx last year and was never heard from again. There was a letter addressed "Dear Mother" that read, "Don't you know slavery is over!" Beryl didn't try to figure out what that was about. And there were little poems on origami paper to Tyrone, and a letter to him saying that when they were sixteen they could quit school, and get their working papers, and then they could get jobs, get married, and move to Los Angeles.

Randy's diary wasn't locked. Beryl had seen it so few times, she'd forgotten all about it. Now here it was in her hot little hands: Randy's whole life story.

Beryl raced through the boring entries—the ones about hating school, or how hard it had rained that day. She was in a hurry for "the good stuff." Like the entry about the day Tyrone kissed her in the elevator. On the lips. And it had felt good. There was the one she wrote about cutting last period and sneaking over to Rhonda's house and drinking some of Rhonda's mother's Scotch. Man, Beryl said to herself, Randy's been *wild!* There were more entries about Tyrone, and one was about more kissing. Beryl flipped and flipped and . . . When she reached the entry for today, her stomach dropped.

"Last night Beryl found out that Daddy's not my real father. She keeps asking me a lot of stupid questions. She's such a pain."

As Beryl was trying to mutter up some vicious come-back, she remembered her mission. She rummaged on through the box, tossing some of Randy's stuff on the floor: another small spiral notebook; a red, black, and green button; unopened letters from Holland; an Afro pick with a fist-shaped handle; favors from birthday parties; the Abracadabra man's book; picture postcards from nobody.

She knew it was him, the minute she saw it. Like Randy, he had large round eyes that darted out at you, and he was also light-skinned, lighter than their mother, just like Randy. Randy was bowlegged, and so was this man. His hair was done in what her father had told her they used to call a "konk": straight and shiny-shiny black, with waves. Beryl remembered that in their album there were photographs of her daddy sporting a konk, too. This man was taller than her father, and maybe a little more handsome, she had to admit. What with his smile and the way he was standing, as if waiting to fast-dance, he looked like a whole lot of fun. His tan-and-white checked suit and brand-new-looking white shoes made her think he might also be rich.

On the back of the photograph was written in a sprawling hand: "To My Darling Ruth. Your True Love, Rusty."

Rusty? What kind of name is *that?* Beryl wrinkled her nose. Rusty? That ain't no name for a mystery man.

"What are you doing in my stuff!"

Beryl hadn't heard the front door close, or the footsteps, or the opening of their bedroom door. But here was Randy almost halfway across the room.

"I just, I—"

"You *broke* it!" Randy's teeth were clenched, like her fists, as she stared down at her busted keepsake box, and her belongings in a jumble on the floor. "You—" Randy snatched Beryl up and sent her smash into the heat pipe, headfirst.

"Ow!" Beryl whined, holding her head in her hands, and trying hard to hold back the tears.

"Good for you," Randy spat as she began to put her things up on her bed. "That's what you get for not minding your own business."

"And that's what you get," Beryl said, pointing down, "for not letting me see his picture. Box wouldn't have gotten broken if you'd . . ."

Randy looked down at the squares of beige-speckled floor between them and saw the photograph. When she looked up, her eyes were empty. Without a word, or so much as an angry huff or sigh, she picked it up, and dropped it into her keepsake box as if it were one of her postcards from nobody.

Beryl found the silence alarming. Randy was going to tell on her for sure. "I'm sorry, Randy, okay?"

"You're sorry all right, a sorry little—"

"You gonna tell?"

"What do you think?" Randy threatened.

"If you do," Beryl said, digging deep to get up her nerve, "then I'll tell about all those bad things you've been doing that I read about in your diary!"

"Just shut up and get away from me, you little brat!"

"Oh, yeah . . . ?" Beryl huffed, "Well, I'd rather be a little brat than a little bastard!"

Randy flinched. For a long minute she just stared at Beryl.

Last tag, Beryl said to herself, feeling pleased and quite proud of herself. She knew what this cuss word meant, just as she knew the other "b" word meant female dog.

How many times had they fought!

With fists.

With sneak-attack slaps.

With picky-pestery pranks.

With "I hate you!" and "Drop dead!"

A hundredthousandmillionthousandhundred times.

But each time, a few hours later or, at most, a whole twenty-four, it was forgotten. Nothing ever really stuck or stabbed; there were never any deep wounds to heal.

But this time?

Randy cut her eyes hard at Beryl, and turned back to putting her things into her keepsake box.

"I didn't mean that . . . I'm sorry." Beryl stepped toward her, whimpering now. "I take it back," she added as she reached to touch Randy's arm.

"Don't touch me!" Randy's tone was so steely Beryl jumped back.

"I said I didn't mean it!" Beryl screamed, tears streaming down her face. "I told you I was sorry!"

"What is going on in here?" Mrs. Nelson stood in the doorway, arms akimbo. As she moved into the room, Beryl rushed to her side sobbing. "She tried to kill me! . . . Look what she did to my head!" Until now, Beryl had forgotten about the pain and hadn't at all felt the knot in the middle of her forehead, steady on the rise.

Seeing the knot, Mrs. Nelson winced for Beryl. "Randy!"

"Yeah, I pushed her and she hit her head." Randy defied her mother's glare, and kept looking straight in her eyes. "But it was an accident, okay?"

"No, it's not okay and why'd you push her?"

"Ask *her*."

"I'm asking *you*, Miranda!"

Randy looked away and pointed to her keepsake box. "This is why I pushed her. When I was up at Grandma's she broke into it and went through my stuff."

"This true, Beryl?"

"You think I'm lying?" Randy yelled.

"You raising your voice to me?" Mrs. Nelson's own

voice was now raised and pitched a little higher in what Beryl called her "fussin' voice."

Mrs. Nelson held Beryl by the shoulders and pushed her out from her. Beryl lowered her eyes. "She called me a shrimp and kicked my crayons," she whimpered, "and then, then, I only just wanted to see his picture 'cause when I asked her to lemme see it she said no."

"What picture?"

"Her real daddy."

"Lord, have mercy," Mrs. Nelson sighed, raising her eyes to the ceiling. Finding no one up there to be annoyed with, she shook her head and sterned her face.

"So because I wouldn't let her see it, she decided to thief her way to it!" Randy spat out.

Beryl was clinging to her mother again, desperate to be out of the spotlight. "And why don't you ask her why she be letting Tyrone kiss her and about how she drinks Rhonda's mother's liquor?"

"What!" Mrs. Nelson exclaimed.

"What seems to be the problem?" asked Mr. Nelson from the doorway.

"Beryl broke into Randy's keepsake box," Mrs. Nelson began rather matter-of-factly. "She wanted to see Rusty's picture."

"Who?"

"Russell Evans, honey," Mrs. Nelson said softly. She didn't need to see her husband's face to know what he was thinking. "If you don't deal with it now," he'd said late last night, "you'll only have to deal with it later."

Rusty's just his nickname, Beryl said to herself. And Evans . . . that would've been Randy's last name had Mommy married him. And mine, too. But then, if she had married him, maybe I wouldn't be Beryl. Maybe my name would be . . . Serena, or Joann. Or maybe my name *would* be Beryl, but I'd be bowlegged. And taller.

". . . and she hit her head on something," Mrs. Nelson was finishing up.

"And what's this about Tyrone giving Randy liquor?"

"No, Tyrone's been giving Randy kisses, the liquor—" Mrs. Nelson broke off, suddenly aware that she had no idea what she was talking about, or what was really going on. "Randy, what is this about Tyrone and liquor?"

"It's nothing," Randy shrugged. "She just musta misunderstood something I wrote in my diary, which she had no business—"

"Which was?" Mrs. Nelson interrupted.

"Just that, uh, one time when I was over Rhonda's house, she asked me to taste some Scotch."

"And you did?"

"Just a little."

"And what possessed you to taste even a little?"

"She asked me to." Randy shrugged again, as if that were a fool question.

"So," Mr. Nelson weighed in, "if Rhonda asked you to jump off a building, I suppose you'd go looking for a cape?"

"No," Randy said, with a little more sass than her behind could afford at the moment. Grown-ups are so dry, she thought. Same old lame lines all the time.

"And what's going on with you and Tyrone?" Mrs. Nelson wanted to know.

"Nothing."

"Nothing? So what's this about kissing?"

"He just kissed me on the cheek," Randy mumbled. "A few times. That's all."

"But you wrote how—" Beryl piped up. Randy shot her a look that said, I will kill you *dead* if you say one more word!

And Beryl wanted to live.

"What I wrote was just pretend stuff," Randy explained. "I write a lot of stuff in my diary that's not true."

"Well, young lady—who'd *bet-ter* remember that we've said she's too young to even *think* about having a boyfriend—" Mrs. Nelson pressed, "let me have a look at some of this pretend stuff."

"Ruth, leave her have her privacy," Mr. Nelson said softly.

"But, Daniel, I want to—"

"Ruth, let it rest for now." His voice was firm, like the look he gave Randy that told her he hadn't bought the lie either. "I'm sure that from now on Randy's going to start thinking twice about the things she pretends with Tyrone, or any other boy."

Randy wanted to say "Thank you," but decided she'd rather stay sullen.

"And as for you," Mr. Nelson said, turning to Beryl, "I'm very disappointed in you. Don't you ever let me hear of you invading Randy's privacy, or anybody else's, for that matter. You hear me?"

"Yes, Daddy," Beryl said, tears on the rise.

"You're getting to be a big girl, and it's time you start acting like one."

"But she—"

"Beryl . . ." Mr. Nelson's voice was getting rumbly.

"But how come I always—"

"Beryl!" Mr. Nelson's voice was now very rumbly. "When's the last time you were on punishment?"

"The other week."

"And you remember how it felt not to be able to go outside for a whole week?"

"Daddy, please don't put me on punishment again," Beryl pleaded. "Can you just give me a little beatin'?"

"If you stop with the lip, I'll let you off with just a warning."

Beryl vowed not to say another word for the rest of the night.

Mr. Nelson turned to leave the room, but then walked toward Randy. "Let me have the box." Randy flinched, feeling betrayed. Determined not to beg or bend, she stiffly handed it over, avoiding his eyes.

"No, take your things out of it," he said. Randy did

so, with a small smile. And this time when she handed over her keepsake box, she looked up at him.

"Where are the little whatamacallits, the, uh, hinges?"

Randy patted around on her bedspread, and then searched the floor. As she did, Mr. Nelson nodded at the screwdriver on Randy's bed and said to Beryl, "Go put that back exactly where you found it and bring me the little hammer."

When Beryl returned with the little hammer, she saw Randy giving Mr. Nelson the hinges, and saying, "Thanks a lot, Daddy."

"Have it fixed in a jif," he assured her.

"What about my head?" Beryl whined, sidling up to her father, her vow of silence not even a memory. "You not gonna put a Band-Aid on it, or rub it with something?"

"It'll be fine with no help from me," he said coolly. " 'Course you'll be looking like a unicorn for a few days but it'll heal down. In the meantime, it'll serve as a reminder that there's a price to pay for wrongdoing. You know what the word 'Consequences' means, right?"

"No," Beryl pouted.

"You don't?" Mr. Nelson rumbled.

"I mean, yes, I know what it means. It's like payback."

As Mr. Nelson moved from the room, Beryl started to follow. But Mrs. Nelson brought her to a stop with, "Uh-uh, Beryl, you stay right here. I want to have a little talk with you and Randy."

7

Mrs. Nelson pulled out the chair to the vanity. As she sat, she motioned for Beryl and Randy to do likewise. Each plopped down at the foot of her bed. They waited as Mrs. Nelson wondered how to begin.

"Now, tell me. What is going on between you two?"

Beryl looked at Randy, who wouldn't look her way. "I just wanted to see his picture, that's all," she finally said in a tiny voice.

"So did you?"

"Yeah."

"You satisfied?"

Beryl dropped her head. "I guess so."

"Randy," Mrs. Nelson said, "give me the picture."

Randy hesitated, remembering her battle to keep it the day she found it.

It was a few years ago, and no ordinary Nelson Saturday morning. The family was full throttle into spring cleaning. Mr. Nelson chomped away at the heavy work—washing the winter grime and gluck from all the windows, double-mopping floors and then hard-waxing them with the Buff-O-Matic he'd bought his wife for her birthday, and the kitchen was going to be repainted. Beryl was his helper, fetching him rags and cleaning supplies, stirring the paint with that special stick, which she imagined would be just the thing to use on a giant's tongue when the doctor said, "Say, Ahh."

Mrs. Nelson had told her family that her mission was to get rid of everything they didn't absolutely need or absolutely cherish, pledging to free her home of every piece of paper, every forgettable memento, everything she'd kept only because it was "too good to throw away." Mr. Nelson, who hated clutter, hastened to pre-pare a variety of boxes and bags for what was to be given away, and what was to be trashed. "We'll do our level best to help you keep your word. Right, girls?"

One of Randy's jobs that day had been to take the boxes and bags of junk out to the incinerator. On one trip, she defied parental guidance and took a lazy man's load. With an armful of different-sized boxes topped by a scruffy brown shopping bag, she eased out of the apartment. Small, tightrope steps she took, careful not to breathe too hard. Within two feet of the incinerator, the bag, then box three, two, one tipped over and down to the floor. There was a certain thrill to the mess. Randy prided herself on having made it as far as she had.

In the spilling of letters, long-ago paid bills, newspaper clippings, and whatnots, a photograph caught her eye. On the back was "Your True Love, Rusty," and instantly she knew this was her father. One of the few facts she had gotten from her mother was his name. Rusty was a likely nickname for Russell.

"And what's taking you so long?" Mrs. Nelson wasn't mad, just anxious to keep the work going briskly along. Before Randy could duck the photograph behind her back, her mother was almost up on her. As Randy started to speak, she lowered her head. She couldn't bring herself to look up at her mother. Eyes scampering around the spilled junk, and the photograph a-swing in her hand, she finally asked, "Is this my father?"

Mrs. Nelson let her eyes drop to Randy's hand and then yanked them away. Her mouth was tight, her eyes out of reach of Randy's gaze. "Why, yes, it is."

"Can I keep it?" Randy asked her mother's stomach.

"No. Now, give me the picture."

"Why can't I just have it?" she asked her mother's outstretched hand.

"I don't see why you would want . . . I mean, you don't really know—"

"But you threw it away, so why can't I have it?" Randy's eyes met her mother's head-on.

"All right, all right, keep it if it makes you feel better, but I really don't see why—"

"What y'all doing?" Beryl called out from the door. Miss Nosy startled them both, and both blinked.

"Just getting all this junk picked up and thrown out," replied Mrs. Nelson, grabbing up a batch to shove down the incinerator's mouth. Randy slid the photo into her back pants pocket, then bent for a scoop of junk herself.

"I'll help!" Beryl skipped down the hall, in a hurry for a chance to send some of the bad-bad garbage down to Hell.

In the days to come Randy would often curl up on her bed and just stare at the photograph. It was always when Beryl wasn't around—not in the room, not able to barge into her mood. After awhile Randy hardly ever looked at the photograph, barely glancing at it while riffling through her keepsakes looking for something else. But she had kept it.

And now, so many, many months later, she didn't want to give it up. What, she wondered, was her mother planning to do with it when she said, "Give me the picture."

Randy blinked. Her arm felt leaden as she handed her mother the photograph.

Mrs. Nelson studied the photograph for awhile, and as she did her face went soft with a gaze that Beryl took to be affection. She's missing him, she shuddered. But Mrs. Nelson wasn't missing the man. Just remembering.

Handing the photograph back to Randy, Mrs. Nelson

said, "Randy, I want you to know that Russell was an all right guy."

Randy couldn't believe she'd gotten the photograph back so easy. After a pause, she timidly asked, "You didn't call him Rusty?"

"Sometimes, but I preferred Russell."

"You like it better than Daniel?" Beryl asked.

"Baby, just because you like one thing doesn't always mean you like another thing less."

"Mommy?" asked Randy, lowering her eyes. "How come you don't talk to me about him?"

"Didn't know you wanted to know anything."

"Yes, you did."

Mrs. Nelson's face flashed indignant. But then her conscience pricked, reminding her of the times she had shoved Randy off the subject with barren words—"Oh, it's so complicated, you wouldn't understand." And commands—"Let's not talk about it." And lies—"It upsets your father." This had always baffled Randy, because Mr. Nelson had never gotten angry the few times she had asked him a question.

The skimpy responses and half-truths and lies made Randy twist up inside, and unsure. Sometimes, when Mr. Nelson got after her about something, or punished her, she wondered if he was really upset with what she'd done or whether it was with what she was. Not his child. And when he was loving and kind and being Daddy all the way around, she sometimes feared it was

72

pity. In most stories she'd read, the stepchild was treated cruelly, or simply ignored. Or maybe everything was going along fine, but then the real parent died and the stepparent changed.

"Lord, have mercy," Mrs. Nelson sighed as she tried to peer into Randy's mind. It wasn't an empty phrase as it was most times. It was a prayer. She was truly asking for mercy, and the right words. "You're right, Randy, you're right," she said softly. "I thought talking about it, about him, would stir up confusion inside you. I kept saying I'd wait 'til you were older to explain things. I was afraid you . . . Sort of like when you were in third grade, and they wanted to skip you. At first I thought, okay, but then some people started saying things like it'd make you half-crazy, or different, and that you might finish school early and very smart, but not well-adjusted."

Randy was puzzled. "But you did let me skip."

"Yeah, but that's because your father told me to stop listening to other people. 'She can handle it,' he said. And he was right." Mrs. Nelson searched her daughter's eyes for she knew not what. "You and Beryl both can probably handle a lot more things than I think, sometimes." She paused for a long minute, and shifted in the chair. "I was about two years older than you, Randy, when I met Russell. He was sweet, and had wide dreams. Wasn't long before we were sure we were meant to be together, forever and ever. We wanted to marry, but Mama wouldn't give her permission."

"She didn't like him?" Randy's head was down now.

"No, that wasn't it. She believed he had . . . potential, was how she put it. But also, she believed I was too young. All me and Russell knew was that we were in love. And what else could matter? Mama just didn't understand, we thought. She couldn't see or feel what we knew. Yet in all, we weren't brazen enough to elope."

Randy thought about her and Tyrone.

"And so," Mrs. Nelson continued, "while we waited, we convinced ourselves that we were already married . . . in our hearts, and didn't need to wait to have . . ."

"S-E-X?" Beryl mumbled.

Neither mother nor daughters were aware that Mr. Nelson was outside the room listening, and with a smile, because he liked what he heard. Truth, and no problems.

"And I got pregnant," Mrs. Nelson continued. "Then things didn't seem so forever and ever. Conversation soon got hard. We didn't feel so sure of ourselves, or of anything, anymore."

Beryl tensed up, waiting for her mother to finish. She didn't want to think about her mother having sadness in her life, about her mother not being strong and together. She did not want to stop being a little mad at her, either.

Most of all, she wanted the rest of the story to *go away*! She wished there was a way life would go back to yesterday. Like on TV when people do that fast-fast, jerky backwards run and the magic person fixes the problem or changes one teeny-tiny thing and then everyone moves forward again like nothing ever happened. Why'd she have to ask that question? Why'd she want to know how long her parents had been married?

Beryl snuck a look at Randy, whose eyes were steady and straight on their mother, waiting, waiting, waiting, for her to talk on.

"Russell wanted to do the right thing by me."

"Marry you?" Randy asked.

"Yes."

"But he did the wrong thing to you?" asked Beryl, looking for reasons not to like this Rusty man.

"No. What he did, or what *we* did rather, was what was best for our situation. And it was Mama that gave us the courage to do that."

"Grandma?" Randy asked. "She didn't put you out the house?"

"Put me out the house? What would make you think that?" Mrs. Nelson was truly puzzled.

"There's a girl at my school . . . her mother beat her bad and threw her out."

"No, Randy, your grandmother wasn't like that. After I told her, she just got quiet, and she stayed that way for half a day."

"Was Granddaddy alive then?" Beryl asked.

"Uh-uh. He passed when I was about your age." Mrs. Nelson was remembering again. Her father, this time.

"Anyway," she continued, "next time Mama had a word to say to me it was to tell me to have Russell come see her. When he did, she sat us down and asked, 'And what is it that you two plan to do?' Russell said, 'I plan to marry Ruth, ma'am.' Then Mama asked, 'Why?' Russell looked at me and I looked at him and neither one of us was too eager to look at Mama. After awhile she said, 'I seen too many young people forced up an aisle just to make everything look all right and roses, and inside of a year they've got nothing to show for the marriage except rage and strife.' "

"So Grandma is to blame for . . ." Randy had always wanted to know who had put the stop on her having things normal. It was easy to paint the zero—him—as the flimflam. She'd heard older girls talk about the kind of guys who did the "wham, bam, thank you ma'am." But why hadn't her mother seen through him in time? Or had her mother been the floozy? Sometimes, for a flicker, she wished she could be unborn and come again into the world to two people who could work things out.

"Blame?" Mrs. Nelson's bittersweet tone made Randy feel as if her search was a preposterous pursuit.

"Well, if Grandma hadn't—"

"Randy, she's not to blame for anything. She helped us be . . . real, as you young folks say. She said, of course, there'd be talk—you know, gossip and rumors—and she said it wouldn't be easy raising a child by myself. She'd be there to help me, she said, whatever decision I made. Russell . . . he finally told me he didn't really want to get married, right away. And then right away became never. On both our parts. Soon after you were born, he left New York. His cousin had found him a good job, he said. And Grandma kept true to her word. She was my rock . . ."

Beryl wondered if her mother wanted to cry.

"Ma, do you know where he lives?" Randy's question had the push of a demand.

"No," Mrs. Nelson started to lie. "What I mean is, I know I have an address somewhere around here, but he may have moved."

"If he hasn't, could I—you think he'd let me see him?" Never had Randy imagined she'd ever ask this question, but it had come out so easy.

"Well, Randy, I can't speak for him. I don't know what his life is like."

During the silence Beryl began imagining movie scenes most melodramatic, co-starring Randy the ingrate taking back all the Father's Day presents she'd given Mr. Nelson and running off to live with her very rich, real father, and she, Beryl, left all alone—but with the bedroom all to herself.

"But tell you what I'll do," Mrs. Nelson finally said. "I'll look for that address tomorrow." Don't put it off, she could hear her husband caution. "Better yet," she added, "why don't I call information and see if he's listed. I can do that now."

Uh-oh, Beryl panicked.

"Would you really?" was Randy's response.

"Yes, Randy, really." Mrs. Nelson's smile was natural. Catching sight of the fright in Beryl's eyes, she said, "Baby, what are you looking so scared about? Everything's going to be all right."

After Mrs. Nelson left the room, Beryl looked over at Randy and started to say something, but held back. Randy stretched out on her stomach with her head at the foot of her bed, her face to the window.

Beryl remained seated at the foot of her bed, swinging her legs ever so slightly. After a minute, she got up and then down to the floor to pick up her drawing pad and the crayons from under her bed. She heard her parents talking in the kitchen. Her father's voice wasn't at all rumbly, and her mother's was sort of high, but it wasn't her fussin' voice. After awhile Beryl heard her mother come down the hall and go into her room. After another while she heard her parents' bedroom door close. Then, her mother was talking.

Beryl tipped up to her parents' bedroom and pressed her ear to the crack between the door and its frame. "Yes, it's been a long time," she heard her mother say. Next, she heard, "What are you doing?"

Mr. Nelson was coming down the hall with Randy's

keepsake box cradled in one arm and the little hammer in his other hand.

Beryl jumped away from the door. "Nothing," she twitched, and then followed him into her room.

"You fixed it!" Randy exclaimed. As she examined the hinges she saw that he'd even blackened in the spots where some of the lacquer had been ripped away.

"Uh-huh," said Mr. Nelson.

Beryl followed her father from the room and to the catchall closet to put away the hammer, and then back up the hall, past her parents' room and into the kitchen. When he turned on the kettle, Beryl asked, "You know who Ma's talking to?"

"Uh-huh," Mr. Nelson replied, reaching in the cabinet for the jar of Maxwell House.

"I'll do it," Beryl volunteered.

She got a cup and saucer from the dish rack, and a spoon. She dipped up a heaping spoonful of coffee, and then, like a chemist preparing a prescription and aware that not enough of this ingredient would make the medicine ineffective and too much would make it poison, she gently shook some of the coffee off and then dropped the spoonful into the cup. She added one level spoon of sugar, just like her father always did. "Can I pour?" she asked when the kettle whistled.

"Not today, popcorn."

"That's what you always say, and you always let Randy do it."

"But she's almost four years older than you and a good bit taller," he said, pouring the boiling water into his cup.

"Do you think I'm going to be short all my life, Daddy? Linda's got a cousin who's seventeen and she says he's the same size he was when he was six."

"Have you grown since you were six?"

"Yeah."

"Then what are you worried about?"

She trailed him into the dinette and sat across from him at the table. She watched him stir, and the steam grow thin.

"Daddy?"

"Yes?"

"Ma's talking to that Rusty man, right?"

"Uh-huh."

At that moment Beryl heard her mother leave her bedroom and go into her and Randy's. After a few minutes, she heard Randy and her mother go into her parents' room, and the door shut.

Beryl shot up from the table. "I'll be right back."

"Where you going?"

"To get my, my drawing pad. I want to show you a picture I made for you, Daddy."

When Beryl reached her parents' room, she pressed her ear to the door.

"What did I tell you about respecting peoples' privacy," said Mr. Nelson, leaning out from the dinette.

"I just wanted to see if . . ."

"If what?" Mr. Nelson beckoned her back into the dinette.

"If Randy was talking to him. Daddy, ain't you scared they gonna leave us?"

"No."

"What if he's rich? And what if Ma wants to take me with them?"

"Beryl, ain't nobody going nowhere. Except for maybe a visit."

8

City heat and crowded lives were only just beginning to jam up the day. The playground was pretty quiet, except for a handful of kids jangling on the monkey bars over here and a few sailing wa-a-ay up in the swings over there.

The handball court Beryl had all to herself.

Pwup. Bounce. Slap. She began with nice-and-easy lobs to the wall and gentle slapbacks. Pwup. Bounce. Slap. Again and again and again, with her right hand growing numb to the sting. Pwup. Bounce. Slap. Pwup, bounce, slap. A little harder meant faster, meant harder, meant faster, meant harder, meant trying to slap the mess out of her confusion and fears.

Pwup bounce slap, pwup bounce slap, pwup bounce slap. Pwupbounceslap. Pwupbounceslap. Pwup-bounceslap. PwupbounceslapPwupbounceslapPwup-bounce-slap. Then, pwupslap, pwupslap, in her challenge to beat the bounce.

And now, for a little practice with her left hand, while nobody was around to laugh.

"I got next winners!" someone wolfed from the basketball court.

Face sporting menace, hard bop in her gait, and shoulders cocked forward, it was Linda doing her imitation of the notorious Priscilla Watson—or Priscilla the Gorilla as she was called behind her back. Other than in her rough, brutish ways, Priscilla Watson bore no resemblance to an ape, and would have been a very attractive girl if she ever wiped the scowl off her face, and learned to stand up straight and step like a queen. But Gorilla rhymed with Priscilla.

"Aaaah!!!" Beryl screamed. "It's Priscilla the Gorilla! Run for your lives!" It was an old routine that never got stale, and never failed to bring both girls to laughter.

But Priscilla the Gorilla wasn't always so funny. One of the big-time bullies from the Johnson projects, she'd beaten many a big boy's behind for ignoring her claim to next winners, and for less. And she was the "monster," as Beryl had put it, who was "killing" Randy a few years ago.

Beryl had been funning it up with back-to-back trips down the sliding board. As she was about to climb the ladder for the hundredth time, a little, thick kid came out of nowhere, pushed in front of her and scampered up the ladder. "Not fair!" Beryl had yelled, as Stubby breezed down the slide, sticking out his tongue at the end of his ride. When Beryl slooped down, she bowled him over with her feet. "Next time you better wait your turn," she warned.

"And next time, you better watch where you're going," Priscilla barked as she swatted Beryl to the ground and helped up Stubby—her cousin, Beryl later found out.

Beryl saw tears, and then Randy to the rescue with, "And next time why don't you pick on somebody your own size?" Then she hoisted Beryl up.

"Oh, yea-a-ah," Priscilla threatened. "And I know that somebody ain't you," she added, shoving Randy in the chest.

"She's my big sister!" Beryl barged in. "And she don't take no stuff!"

Randy was indeed a brave little something, but with Priscilla Watson in her face, she was wishing Beryl had kept this brag to herself.

"Oh, yea-a-ah," Priscilla taunted again, with another shove at Randy. And then again. "And when I finish beating the mess out of you, I'll be ready for your mother!"

Who hit whom first was beside the point, and because Randy and Priscilla were at it so quick it was impossible to tell. Not a soul jumped in to break it up. The growing crowd only threw up cheers and jeers typical of cowards and fools, as they spectated the punching, the kicking, the scratching, the missed lunges and swipes and swings, and the kneeing and the grabs at hair, and the screaming, the screaming, the screaming.

And Beryl?

She was the screaming. "HELP! That monster is killing my sister! Somebody, HELP!"

Before too long Bullwinkle broke through the crowd, with four long bleats of his whistle. "All right, break it up!" he shouted. "I said break it up, RIGHT NOW, or I'm taking you in!"

Taking them in? He wasn't a cop, just a security guard who could, at most, make them sit in the guardhouse to cool off or sweat over the threat of a parent being called. But he, with his squinty eyes, tall, gangly, moose-face self was more frightening than a cop. He was the meanest guard in the complex. He never looked the other way when you cut across the grass, or littered, or even looked as if you were about to fight. Bullwinkle took his job very seriously. When he yanked Priscilla off her sister, Beryl was ever so very glad that he did.

Although Randy emerged with a bloody knee and a cut above her eye and aches she wouldn't feel until tomorrow, and Priscilla with only a few slim scratches, it was Randy the crowd declared (to themselves) the victor. She was one of the few girls who had ever fought back against Priscilla the Gorilla. And she'd done it for her little sister. Beryl was in awe as she skipped alongside her on their silent way home.

"What's wrong with you?" Linda was entering the handball court and seeing Beryl's face so sad.

In the short tick of time it had taken Linda to get there, Beryl had relived not only that fight, but flashes of so many good, sweet, crazy-fun, and proud times she'd had with her sister. Like Randy showing her how to work a skate key, and how to do the box stitch. Randy holding her tight on the Wild Mouse and in the haunted house at Coney Island. Randy helping her make her S's less and less like sailboats when she was learning script. Randy putting Noxzema all over her face and wilding out her hair and creeping into their night-dark room in a game of "Witch." There wasn't a snippet of all the nasty pranks Randy had pulled, or all the times she'd teased Beryl to tears. And now, Beryl feared there'd be no more good times.

"And what happened to your head?" Linda asked, now face-to-face with Beryl.

"Me and Randy had a, a problem, as my daddy would say."

"She look like a unicorn, too?" Linda snickered.

Beryl tried to sound tough. "Shut up and serve." She tossed Linda the handball and backstepped to the center of the court.

Pwup. Bounce.

"What'd y'all fight about?"

Linda's serve sent Beryl sideskipping quick to the right. Slap.

"We, uh . . . Aw, it was nothing."

Pwup. Bounce . . . Linda's slap was nice and easy, and dead center. Beryl flew forward and managed a hit, left and low. But Linda had guessed right, and was on the mark, ready with a hard hit, not to the right, as Beryl had expected, but a little to Linda's left. Beryl dashed over, left hand braced to swat the ball with all her might. It zoomed way over to the right, but not too fast for Linda to meet it with a hard slap—before the first bounce. By the time Beryl neared the ball it had bounced once and was on its way to the back fence.

"One, zip," Linda called out as she trotted over to the ball now rolling around center court.

The sun was playing peek-a-boo with dark clouds, but Beryl and Linda weren't paying the weather any mind. They were aware only of the cement wall, the boundary lines, and the peachy-pink Spalding. Soon they weren't even Beryl and Linda, but two sets of unfeeling hands that had become extensions of darting eyes, and two sets of crouch and spring-ready legs joined to two sets of sneakered feet poised to scissorstep, sprint, stop, pivot, and dash.

Pwup, bounce, slap. Pwupbounceslap. Pwup. Bounce . . .

The high bounce had Beryl trotting backwards and

then up off the ground for a hard high five with the ball, and then stumbling back into the fence. The ball hung in the air too long, petering out a few inches from the wall.

"Twenty-one, seventeen," Linda announced, arms jutted up like a triumphant boxer.

Beryl was still sagging against the fence. The minute the ball left her hand she'd felt how weak her hit had been and known the game was over.

"Ready when you are," Linda said, dribbling the ball.

"Naw, let's do something else."

"We just started. What, you a sore loser?"

"No, I'm not a sore loser. I just don't—"

"I'll let you serve first."

"Naw, I just don't feel like another game right now, that's all."

"Dag, what's wrong with you?"

"Nothing, I just . . ." Beryl sat down on the concrete ledge at the base of the fence, feet flat, knees bent. "Linda, you ever found out something that you couldn't . . . that didn't . . . If I tell you something you promise not to tell nobody?"

"Cross my heart and hope to die," Linda said, with a little snatch of the bugaloo.

"Come on, I'm serious."

"Yeah, yeah, yeah, I promise," Linda yanged, as she joined Beryl at the fence. Beryl now had her knees pressed to her chest, and was hugging her legs as if she were cold. When Linda sat down she let her legs sprawl out before her in a wide vee.

"I just found out that my daddy's not Randy's real father . . ." Beryl looked at Linda for a moment, for a response, a reaction that did not come. "He's some man named Rusty, and he lives in Philadelphia."

"Does Randy know?"

"That he lives in Philadelphia?"

"No, that your father—"

"Yeah, she's *been* known, since she was a little kid. *I'm* the only one who didn't know until the other day . . . And now everything's all funny."

"What you mean, funny?"

"Since I found out, Randy's been acting real strange. Hinkty. She won't talk to me about it and . . . I don't know, it's like she hates me."

"Why would she be hating you?"

"Maybe she's jealous, because I got my real daddy and she don't."

"But you say she been known, so if she was gonna be jealous and hating you she'd have been doing that stuff for a long time."

"But now that she knows I know, she knows I—You getting me all mixed up. Anyway, things feel different. Like my family ain't the same and is all messed up."

"What you talking about?" Linda huffed. "Your family ain't all messed up. I mean, y'all live over here in Stevenson Plaza, with elevators and stuff. And your mother's always home. And I never see your father a lot, but when I do he always looks like he's . . . like he ain't going nowhere." She bounced the Spalding a time or two. "Whenever my father comes around, all he says is the same dumb thing: 'How's my little girl?' Gives me some money, and splits, talking 'bout 'See you soon.' Yeah, right. . . . And I'm always wishing I had a sister. A big sister would be the coolest."

"But Randy's just a half-sister. It's like we're not the same thing. Know what I mean?"

"No. And I wouldn't care if she was a quarter sister. I'd be glad to have any kind of sister."

"Yeah," Beryl sighed, eyes traveling over to Linda's Pro-Keds, "but you only children get a lot of stuff."

"I'd still rather have a sister."

Beryl thought about what Linda said. Yes, she'd rather have Randy than a pair of Pro-Keds.

"Linda?"

"Huh?"

"You ever think of going to live with your father?"

"For what? I've never even spent the weekend with him."

"Last night Ma called Randy's real father, and she let Randy talk to him. Randy won't tell me what they talked about, only that she's gonna go see him when we get back from Down South."

"When are you going away?"

"Wednesday. And this morning when I asked Randy

some questions she said she didn't want to talk about it, and maybe she'll go live with him because I'm such a pest."

"Aw, she's probably just trying to psyche your mind. Bet you a dollar she won't go live with him."

"But she said—"

"Did she ever live with him?"

"No. Ma and Daddy got married when she was a real little baby."

"So if your father's been her father for so long, why would she want to leave? Besides, your mother wouldn't let her, I bet."

"But you know, you can quit school at sixteen and get your working papers and then get a job and do what you want."

"We can quit school at sixteen?"

"You didn't know that?" Beryl answered, as if she'd been hip to this for years.

"Hi, Beryl. Hi, Linda."

Over their shoulders they saw Bridget Cherry with her dirty-white poodle, Feather, prancing alongside. Both Beryl's and Linda's "Hi, Bridget" were on the dry side.

Bridget was all right, sometimes: when she was letting them play with her hula-hoop or other toys and games neither of them had, or when she had a birthday party, or a lot of bubble gum. But most of the time . . . like when she tried to play handball and would skip around the court, afraid to hit the ball hard because "Mother said I could get a callous." And like the way she'd flounce her long, light-brown hair, and tell you for the hundredth time that her great-grandfather was a German, as if that was something to be so proud about.

Bridget looped Feather's leash around the arm of the bench that faced the back of the handball court and walked over to the fence.

"Hey, Bridget," Linda called out, over her shoulder. "Is it true you can quit school at sixteen?"

"I think so," Bridget answered, nose just through one of the squares of the fencing. "But only if you have your parents' permission, I think."

"What if you don't?" Linda wanted to know next.

"They put you in jail. At least I think that's what Mother told me. Why? You know someone who wants to quit school?"

"I was just wondering, because Beryl was saying that if her mother didn't let Randy go live with her father—"

"Linda!" Beryl scolded under her breath.

"Oops," Linda whispered back.

"Randy go live with her father?" Bridget ooohed and gasped, "Oh, Beryl, your parents are getting a divorce?" Bridget's tone was so like a statement and so serious that Beryl almost gasped back, "They are?"

"No, my parents aren't divorcing." Beryl shook her head.

"Then . . . ?" Bridget was wondering.

With her eyes, Beryl again scolded Linda, who mouthed a quick "I'm sorry." Meanwhile, Bridget was putting two and two together and coming to the conclusion that there was something not quite right with the Nelson four.

"You mean you and Randy have different fathers?" Bridget whispered.

"Uh-huh," Beryl responded, head hung down.

"So your mother's *already* been divorced?"

"No," Beryl mumbled.

"No?" Bridget frowned. Then came a solemn, hush-hush, "Oh! I See-ee-e."

"You sound like she said somebody died," Linda snapped, turning to face Bridget.

"It's just that, well, you know . . ." Bridget trailed off, imagining the look on her mother's face when she told her that Mrs. Nelson had been a tramp.

"You promise not to tell anybody?" Beryl implored. She, too, was now facing Bridget.

"Not a soul," Bridget whispered.

"Why should it be such a secret?" Linda was almost shouting. "It's not like it's a big deal."

"You know," Bridget said, squatting down right in front of Beryl, "Mother has a cousin who had a baby before she was married and she suffered all her life. Mavis was her name, and when her father found out she was pregnant, you know what he said?"

"What?" asked Beryl in a hushed voice.

"He said that as far as he was concerned his daughter was dead."

Beryl wasn't clear on exactly what Bridget's point was, but she knew her mother was being insulted. "Well, my mother's father was dead when my mother got pregnant with Randy and my grandmother said my mother didn't have to get married because it wouldn't make everything rosy."

Bridget wasn't sure what Beryl had said, but caught enough of it to be shocked. "She *did*?"

Beryl swallowed and nodded.

"Hmmmm," said Bridget. "Well, the whole, whole family got very mad at Mavis. Mother said everybody stopped inviting her to the big family dinners, and some even took her pictures out of their albums."

"Dag," Linda sucked her teeth. "You sure got a snooty-snotty family."

"They're not," Bridget protested. "But Mother says that's what Mavis got for being a tramp and bringing shame on the family." After a long "so there!" look at Linda, Bridget turned to Beryl and asked, "Does Randy know she's a b-a-s-t-a-r-d?"

"Bridget, don't say that," Beryl frowned.

And Linda jumped in with "Because Randy's just Randy and it doesn't matter—"

Bridget cut Linda off with, "But it's true. For your information, Linda, b-a-s-t-a-r-d means an illegitimate child."

Linda was on her feet now. "I know what it means, Miss Priss," she scowled.

Had there not been a fence between her and Linda, Bridget would have shut up. But there was, so she didn't.

"And that means Beryl's mother could have gone to jail . . . I think. She could also have ended up in the crazy house like Mother's cousin. And, you know, the baby died. And Mother said maybe that was best, because at least the child didn't have to live a whole life with the shame of being a b-a-s—"

"Bridget, you should—" Beryl broke in.

"Shut your mouth and mind your own business," Linda finished, with a swift kick to the fence.

Bridget fell back onto the ground, and little Feather started yelping. "What'd I say wrong?" Bridget pouted as she got up and brushed herself off. "I'm just telling you what Mother told me, so I could understand why you're not supposed to have babies before you get married. And anyway, Randy didn't die and your mother's not in the crazy house, or jail, so . . ." Bridget didn't like the way Beryl and Linda were eyeing her. "So, I got to go now," she said, with a flounce of her hair.

As Bridget went for Feather, and then on her merry way, Beryl looked at Linda, who was looking away.

"Muh-ther said," Linda mocked as she sat back down on the ground. "She makes me sick. How can you be friends with her?"

"She's your friend, too, sometimes."

"Not as much as she's yours."

It was one of those sudden thunderstorms, and the devil was beating his wife.

Without a word to one another, Beryl and Linda sprang up and ran from the handball court, cutting across the basketball court to the walkway that ran along the side of Beryl's building.

Beryl loved to be out in rains like this. The pelt of the rainplops felt good, and because there was sun she wasn't filled with dread. But all the windows of their apartment faced the playground, and she knew that her mother was watching to see if she was running right home, as she'd been told, or "taking your sweet time so you could get struck by lightning?"

After Beryl and Linda flew up the steps to the building, they leaned against the front door to catch their breath.

"You want to come up?" Beryl asked as she pressed the buzzer.

"No, I'ma go home."

"Who is it?" Mrs. Nelson trilled through the intercom.

"Me, Ma!"

Bzzzzzz.

Beryl pushed the door open, and said, "Maybe I'll see you later. If it stops raining, come ring my bell."

"Okay," said Linda, as she started down the ramp.

When Linda was halfway down the ramp, Beryl called out, "Linda?"

"Yeah?"

"I was wondering . . ." With one foot in the door, and the rest of her stretched as far forward as she could get, Beryl asked, "Did your parents used to be married?"

"No," Linda clipped. "Why?"

"Just wondering, that's all." With a nervous smile, Beryl added, "You know, Bridget makes me sick, too."

Linda just shrugged and kept on down the ramp, never looking back.

Beryl watched her trot up the street and into her building. Then she remained in the doorway seeing only the rain.

Did a lot of people not grow up with both their parents? Beryl thought about her friends. Stella's father had died, she knew, and that was sad. Debbie was always telling her that her mother was going to put her father out, and that she wished he'd drop dead. And that was sad, too.

No wonder Linda didn't think it was a big deal that her mother hadn't been married when she had Randy. Beryl worried that she'd hurt Linda's feelings, and she was glad she'd not told her she'd called Randy that bad word. And no wonder Linda was talking as if Beryl had the perfect family. This had been the most Beryl had heard Linda say about her father. Somehow the subject had never come up. Or had it? Had she always known that Linda wanted to have a father in every day of her life, and forgotten—because it had nothing to do with her, and because Miss Hazel seemed like the best mother in the world and so what more could Linda want?

And did growing up with both your real parents make you lucky? Special? Was this one of the blessings she was supposed to be counting? If so, was Randy unblessed?

9

Mrs. Nelson was standing in the apartment door with a towel over her shoulder. "I see you ran right home," she smiled as Beryl passed into the apartment. "Grandma called a little while ago," Mrs. Nelson continued as Beryl removed her socks and sneakers. "She wants you to try on the things she's made for you. I told her you'd be up after dinner, but you might as well go now—after you change."

"Okay." Beryl took the towel from her mother and made swift use of it before she went into her room.

Randy was there, with too many clothes laid out on her bed, and a suitcase almost full.

Beryl froze in the doorway. Just that quickly she'd forgotten about the trip Down South, which wasn't what was uppermost in her mind these days.

Randy didn't even look up when Beryl entered the room. Randy was a master at the silent treatment. Since last night, they'd exchanged less than two dozen words, more than half of which were Beryl's.

"Why you packing now?" Beryl wanted to know for-sure, for-sure that Randy wasn't packing for Phila-delphia.

"Because."

"I got to pack today?"

Randy shrugged. Then she taunted. "But I'm sure you can wait till tomorrow because you'll be around. I won't."

"Where you going?"

"Rhonda's in a play. She wants me to help her go over her part in the morning, and then in the afternoon I'll be at the play. And on Wednesday they'll be doing the play again, and after it there's a little party, so by the time I get home, I'll only have time for the last minute things."

Randy was talking to her again? Just like that? Was she really finished being mad at her? "At Harambee House?" Beryl asked, real friendly like.

"Uh-huh." Randy was sort of friendly sounding, too, now.

Harambee House was such an exciting place. The few times Randy had let her come along, Beryl had left wanting an Afro, too. There was bongo music and pic-tures everywhere. All the grownups let you call them by their first name, and most had names that sounded so brave: Akili, Dakari, Jabulani, Kwame, Monifa. And they called her sister—just like that. Efua, the story-telling lady with the wonderfully colorful, long dress and the silver bracelets up to her elbows, called Beryl "my little sister," and had given her a book about Africa. Maybe Efua would be at the play.

"Can I come?" Beryl was practically pleading.

"No," Randy clipped. "It's not for children," she added, promptly returning to her silence, and her packing.

Beryl gritted her teeth. If she thinks I'm gonna beg, she muttered in her mind, she's got another think coming! Beryl changed her clothes with her back to Randy, who didn't even look up when Beryl left the room.

"Okay, I'm going to Grandma's now," Beryl shouted up the hall.

What was taking the elevator so long, Beryl complained, tempted to take the stairs, but deciding against it. She wasn't being good, but smart. Even though her mother forbid her to take the stairs, Beryl sometimes did it, when she went to Stella's or Debbie's house. But taking the steps to Grandma's could mean trouble, because her mother was probably on the phone with her right now, telling her that Beryl was on her way up, which meant Grandma would be waiting at her open door when she got to the floor. Grandma's apartment was the first one off the elevator.

"What happened to your head?" Grandma asked as Beryl stepped off the elevator.

"I know, Grandma, I know," Beryl sighed. "I look like a unicorn."

Beryl found her new clothes draped over the arms and back of the wing chair in the living room. She especially brightened at the sight of the yellow jumper with huge black dots, the white dress with the sailor collar trimmed with red rickrack, and the two pairs of pedal pushers—one a hot green, the other a mild blue. "Thanks, Grandma." Fingering the pedal pushers, she added, "Can't wait to wear these."

"Welcome, sweets. But, now, you want to tell me why you show up at my door looking like somebody's sucked all the red off your lollipop?" Grandma sat down on the sofa and patted the cushion for Beryl to join her.

"Grandma . . ." She plopped down with a sigh. "I'm so tired of being young. Does it get better when you get grown?"

"No. But your handling of things will. If, that is, you make it a policy to learn from your mistakes and keep record of your blessings."

Didn't Grandma know she was only confusing her more? "Grandma . . .?"

"Yesss?"

Beryl hadn't felt this cry coming on. Through her

tears she poured out all that was in her heart—in bits and scrambled pieces, and not making a whole lot of sense, except to someone who loved her. "Nobody told me . . . and Bridget said you could go crazy, and then Linda . . . I think I hurt her feelings. I didn't know she . . . And I'm scared Randy's gonna leave us."

"There, there," Grandma said softly as she put an arm around Beryl. "First of all, Randy's not going to leave y'all. And as for—"

"But I . . ." Beryl continued through sniffles, "I called her a terrible name and she's never gonna forgive me . . . And then I hit my head." Beryl leaned into Grandma, ready to sob it up and get one of those good ole hugs she was always good for.

But Grandma sat Beryl up straight, and her voice was no longer soft. "And what's this name you called her?"

"It's like a cuss word, sometimes. Starts with a b. It's not the word for a lady dog."

"If you mean the word I think you mean, I don't much blame Randy for taking offense."

"But Grandma—"

"You know, I've heard your mind's been on a roll these last few days."

"Ma told you?"

"Sure did."

"About everything?"

"Pretty much, I suppose."

"She tells everybody everything except me," Beryl mumbled. Then, a little louder, "You wasn't mad at Ma for getting pregnant?"

"Well, I was . . . let's say I was more scared for her. I admit, at first, it was a blow, but soon I realized being mad wasn't much going to help."

"But she had done a bad thing!"

Grandma paused. "Yes, Beryl, your mother had done a bad, bad thing, and she's a wicked, wicked person."

Beryl was speechless.

"Now, is that what you wanted to hear? Are you satisfied? Does that make you feel better? And the next time you do a bad thing, do you want all of us to hold it against you, forever?"

Beryl was not feeling better, just wanting to cry. "But Grandma, why—"

"Why? How? What if? . . . All this wondering, what do you think it's going to get you? So now you know something you didn't know before. You got a peek at the way life isn't always so neat and like a storybook. But just because things aren't as you'd thought they were doesn't mean anything has to be different. Unless you choose to make it that way."

"I'm just all confused a little." Beryl was wiping the wet from her face. "Like on Sunday, Pastor Stone was preaching about the part in the Bible that says you're supposed to keep secrets and not be running your mouth. But I don't see how it could be right to keep things from your family." She took a deep breath to fight back more tears.

"Sometimes it's not a matter of right, but of the right time."

"So when did Ma think would be the right time?"

"I can't answer that, but I guess she was waiting for a time when she thought you could handle it. And wouldn't you agree that you're not handling things so well right now?"

"She kinda explained about it last night. But, she's always telling us to be good girls and that it's wrong to—" Tears did trickle then.

"Baby, good and perfect are two different things."

Beryl tried to hold that thought in her mind, but it was too big. "Pastor Stone said God hates gossips more than fools. Was it wrong for me to tell Linda? She's my friend. Only I didn't think she'd blab it to Bridget." Beryl told Grandma about the entire handball court conversation, leaving out no details.

When Beryl was through, Grandma just shook her head and laughed.

"What's so funny?" Beryl whined.

"Baby, I'm not laughing at you," Grandma chuckled, as she rose from the sofa. "I just hope that taught you a lesson about how confusion can and does start."

Beryl sat still and puzzled. The only movement was her eyes following Grandma as she made her way across the room and into the kitchen. She allowed a small smile when Grandma returned, with a glass of ginger ale. Beryl took a big gulp and a deep breath.

"Beryl, I know you been very busy being mad and muddled and feeling left out, but in all of this did you ever once stop to think where you'd be if your mama had married Randy's father?"

"No—"

"—where."

"Huh?"

"That's right," said Grandma, her tone much more serious than before. "You'd be nowhere to be found—not the Beryl I know. Your mommy would have never met, let alone married, the man who is today your daddy." Grandma paused to let her words sink in. Then, with a smile, she added, "And today I might not have no little wild-minded grandbaby like you."

Beryl smiled back. "Can I have some more soda?"

"In a minute. There's just one more thing I want you to think about."

Oh, no, Beryl thought.

"Sometimes it's a good thing to clear the air. And to question. Comes a point, though, when you have to move on, let it go."

As vague as Grandma was, Beryl sensed that she knew what she meant. "But how?"

"Have you talked to the Lord about it?"

Talked to the Lord about it? Beryl had never once thought about prayer. Not for something like this. What would she say? What would she ask for? It wasn't like she needed a sea parted, or wanted a new pair of skates. She had prayed for a whole week for Pro-Keds.

"Any and every burden . . . God cares." Grandma's pause lasted much longer this time. When she broke the silence, she helped Beryl pick up a new mood with, "Do you think you could use a little pocket money while you're Down South?" After Beryl's rapid nod, she said, "Go get my purse there, from the table."

Beryl was to the dinette and back in a flash.

"I was going to wait and give this to you closer to your leaving." Grandma brought two fives from her bag.

"Thanks, Grandma!" Beryl plucked up the money. "I promise I'll save it all for Down South."

"Now, one of those is for Randy. And don't spend it all in one place."

"I won't, and I'll bring you back a souvenir." Then, eyes scooting to the wing chair, she asked, "Can I try on my clothes now?"

Zooming in on the pedal pushers, Beryl was already seeing herself looking boss during her days Down South.

10

They left after midnight.

"More free road," Mr. Nelson had explained. "Night driving saves a lot of wear and tear on your mind." And the journey would be almost twenty hours long.

For Beryl, who had never been any farther south than New Jersey, it would be quite a small adventure. She pleaded to sit up front from the start. Her father called it "ridin' shotgun."

The first thing she had to do was write down the number on the odometer on the pad her father handed her. Across the top of another page, Beryl wrote GAS. Mr. Nelson would fill up in New Jersey, and he reckoned he'd need to do so twice or thrice more before it was all over. FOOD is what she printed on the next page; they'd stop at Maryland House for breakfast; there'd be snacks from other places along the way. Beryl didn't have to ask why she was making these lists. She was used to her daddy keeping track of his money.

She'd have to be ready to hand him the ticket and the toll money when they left the turnpike, keep a sharp lookout for certain highway signs, and check in on the odometer every so often, so she'd know how many miles they'd traveled. She'd have to be ready at a moment's notice to hand him the map, or follow his black ink trail so she could tell him when such-and-such a town was coming up. It'd have to be quick, her father warned.

"Can't keep the inside light on for too long."

"Why?"

"A hazard to other drivers."

For a long while there was just darkness and highway hum, and southbound red lights signaling the curves and straights of the road, and bright whites making for North. And the air was cool, and a little moist.

When Beryl turned to the back seat to announce, "Welcome to Pennsylvania," she found Randy and her mother fast asleep. They stayed that way through all of Pennsylvania, and Beryl bet they'd miss out on Delaware, too.

For long minutes Beryl and her father talked about the ways of driving and roads, and about the relatives she'd be meeting. Then there'd be spells of silence, until Beryl came up with a stretch of questions.

"Who's the oldest of all your brothers and sisters? . . . Is Aunt Cleo the one who sent us that big salty ham last Christmas? . . . The sign with the crooked arrow stands

for what? . . . Are any cousins gonna be my age? . . .
Aren't you scared a cop's gonna catch you speeding? . . .
How come you didn't stay in South Carolina like the
rest of your family? . . . Do you remember your father
at all? . . . How old were you when your mother died?
. . . Here's another upside-down triangle. That means
yield, right? . . ."

Does everybody know? Beryl kept this question to
herself. It was a family reunion. Everybody would be
talking about family stuff. Would they be talking about
Randy?

The fast, cool air rushing through her father's window, open just a crack, would whir, and sometimes
whistle. At times, there was a queer sputtery sound. To
the side, nothing new to see now. Just more and more
and more silhouettes of trees and houses in a darkness
dotted with lights smiling from high up above, and star-
ing coldly, on the right, on the left, out in front.

"Daddy . . ." It was her secret-agent voice. In one
scoot she was close-close to her father. The only thing
between them was his thermos of coffee.

She was talking to the steering wheel when she asked,
"If me and Randy were both about to starve to death
and you only had one hot dog, who would you give it
to?" She held her breath, hoping to hear him think.

"To you both."

"But you only got *one* hot dog, Daddy."

"I'd cut it in two."

"Stop it, Daddy, you know what I mean."

"No. Can't say I do, really."

"I mean, what if . . . what if, like, *I* was dying and Randy was dying too—at the same time—and to live we both needed a blood confusion—"

Mr. Nelson choked a little, trying to stifle his laugh.

"Come on, Daddy, you know what I mean."

"You mean blood transfusion, popcorn?"

"Yeah, that thing. And so, it's like both of us are dying *real* bad, and gonna keep dying to death if we don't get that new blood and—but remember now, there's only *one* bottle of blood—and the doctor says it'll take the *whole* bottle for one of us to live. So you can't split it, Daddy."

"Uh-huh, and?"

"Well, you know . . . which one of us would you tell the doctor to give it to?"

After a full sigh and a short pause, Mr. Nelson answered, "To you."

"Really?" The rush of joy had her sitting up straight, but then came a feeling most uneasy, because she realized that he'd chosen to let Randy—

"And I'd tell the doctor I'd give a bottle of blood for Randy."

What a relief! But of course now she was back where she started. "Dag, Daddy." She shifted over to her side of the car, slumped down in her seat, arms crossed over her stomach. "But that's *not* how the story goes," she whined.

"Why not? We're making it up, aren't we?"

"But . . ." This wasn't going the way she wanted it to go, but at least she didn't have to feel guilty about Randy dying instead of her. Then suddenly it dawned on her that perhaps she had won. "But you'd give me the first bottle. You'd tell the doctor to save me first because you love—"

"Because Randy's a little stronger than you, being bigger and all. So I'd have to figure she could hang on a while longer, until the doctor drew a bottle of blood from me."

"But what if the doctor said that, that . . ." She strained for another what-if he couldn't wiggle out of, and leave her feeling angry and stupid, like now.

"Beryl?"

"Yeah."

"You want to tell me why you're still letting this thing bother you?"

Beryl hugged herself tighter. If he wasn't going to play fair, she wouldn't either. "No."

"Okay. Have it your way. All I know is, you best not be holding onto an attitude when we get to Cleo's."

"How long I got?"

"Stop being fresh." That was her mother. When did *she* wake up?

Beryl leaned her head against the window, and hoped and waited for her mother to go back to sleep, for when it would be safe to ask questions again. It wasn't long before that moment came, but by then Beryl was feeling too tight-headed to come up with any more what-ifs for her father. Her questions were meandering ones, about road signs and any easy thing that popped in her mind.

"No, we don't have to stay awake for the whole trip," said Mr. Nelson in response to Beryl's last question. "Somewhere around Raleigh I'll pull over and take a doze. When we start up again, it'll be Randy's turn to ride shotgun, and then you can take a sleep. And how 'bout we let your mother sit up front for the last leg of journey?" After a pause he added, "If you're feeling sleepy you can go ahead and take a little nap now."

"But you need me."

"Yeah, but I think I can manage alone for the next few hours."

Though her eyes were getting grainy, Beryl strained to stay awake. Maybe he *could* manage without her. Even so, she wanted to watch the darkness when it began to blue, and catch the first light of the rising of the sun.

The sun was long gone when they pulled up to Aunt Cleo's and Uncle Jesse's wide, blue-gray barnlike house with a wraparound porch and nothing close by but

grassland, and a lot of night with lightning bugs wink-
ing, with crickets leapfrogging each other's whistly
chirps, with the ardent smell of rain-fresh earth. A gang
of moths were in a fussy flutter around the porch light.

Aunt Cleo and Uncle Jesse were through the screen
door before the car doors slammed. Aunt Cleo all but
flew down the steps like she'd just won a million-dollar
prize. "Ruth, girl, don't you age? . . . Randy! What a
good-looker you will surely grow up to be!"

Aunt Cleo was a big-boned woman, hair gray all
through and with an almost hawklike face. And so tall,
Beryl marveled. And strong like a man! Beryl found out
when her turn came for some sugar and a crush of a
hug. "And you, little button, last time I saw you, you
weren't but a slat above my knee!"

Aunt Cleo saved her best hug for her brother. "Danny
boy, Danny boy!" was all she could manage through the
tears. And after that, there was another round of sugar
and hugs.

Uncle Jesse was on the smooth and quiet side. He had
warm words, too, but you could breathe through his
hugs. Once around was enough for him. Then he did
the practical thing: went for the luggage and carried it
inside.

Inside, Beryl was struck by the sound and the smell
of clean. Aunt Cleo used the same lemony furniture pol-
ish as her mother, she bet. But Beryl really had no time
to take in the scene because Aunt Cleo was moving

them on through the parlor, and then through the dining room.

"I know y'all must be way past ready for some real food after your journey," said Aunt Cleo as she shepherded them into the kitchen.

"Cleo!" Mrs. Nelson exclaimed. "You better not have gone through any trouble on our account."

"What trouble?" Aunt Cleo pshawed. "Just a little snack."

The platter of fried chicken was picked clean before long, and the plate of biscuits was soon little more than a scattering of crumbs. Mrs. Nelson begged her sister-in-law not to bother heating up the apple pie, but Aunt Cleo's response was "What bother?" And she put black cherries in her nieces' tall glasses of iced tea.

Beryl wanted to stay up on this, her first, Southern night. She wanted to listen to her parents and aunt and uncle talking, talking, talking around the kitchen table. She wanted to keep feeling special, which is how Aunt Cleo made her feel, the way she kept cupping her face in her hands or squeezing her up and sounding like she'd let her have anything she wanted.

But Beryl's head wouldn't hold up, and with one foot in a dream, she couldn't resist at all when her mother led her upstairs, helped her get undressed and in between the crisp, cool sheets of a very plump bed.

At some point Beryl felt herself being gently shaken.

"Mommy?" she purred.

"Move over, will ya?"

Beryl rolled over and over and over so far that she tumbled out of the bed.

"Ooh-owww," she whined, struggling to break through the fog of sleep, to sit up. But the limpness overcame her. And a chill. Then she felt herself being lifted up. Then she was on softness; then, under something smooth.

"My head . . ." Beryl moaned.

"You hurt your head?" a voice asked, as a hand rubbed her head.

"Unicorns . . . gonna get me," Beryl mumbled.

"You okay?" She was being gently shaken again.

"Uh-huh," Beryl purred. "But it's cold . . ."

Beryl was warmer soon, as she felt herself pulled toward more warmth, and the weight of an arm across her body.

11

There'd be plenty of time next week for scouting around the town of his growing up, her father assured her. Today was for getting stretched out from the drive, and waiting for the in-town family to drop by with "welcome home's" and the out-of-towners to check in.

Doing nothing much had never been so easygoing, and gentling.

Beryl had a good time watching Aunt Cleo fuss her mother out of her kitchen after breakfast, telling her to rest herself, and calling her "Sister" every other time . . .

. . . and listening to her daddy talk about old times and new news, and him talking word after word like he'd never left home . . .

. . . and rocking in the red glider on the front porch amazed by so much free sky . . . and tipping into the kitchen in search of a leftover drop biscuit . . .

. . . and walking with her mother far back behind the house to visit the woods, and hearing her mother wish she had less city in her life, and watching her mother looking at her like there was something she wanted to say, leaving Beryl feeling a little closer to her mother, and with a small yearning to tell her she was sorry . . .

. . . and watching for a rabbit or a deer, a raccoon, a possum because Uncle Jesse had said they ran wild out yonder . . .

. . . and wondering how close was yonder.

So what if some Cousin Jimmy had taken Randy out in his car, so he could show off his "New York cousin"—like she wasn't from New York too!

And it was like going to the movies or a museum when Aunt Cleo took her and her mother through her albums to meet more of the family. Some Beryl had met in their album at home. A few others, she was told, had met her years ago when they'd made a visit Up North.

There was her great-grandfather with a tall black hat and a black suit with highwater pants, and her grandparents with their first six children and her father not yet born. A few flips along, there was her father in a sailor suit looking lost; and there he was again and again, growing up. And there was Aunt Cleo young and skinny as a rail looking cow-eyed at a tall, just as skinny, man. "That's Uncle Jesse!" Beryl exclaimed. It had never occurred to her that he might have once had hair and no big belly. "And this is Bunny," Aunt Cleo recounted, "in the Easter pageant. D-boy, you remember how she forgot her poem and just stood stock-still, grinning like a chessy cat, and then Mama whispering out the first line, and Bunny catching on and just speed-racing through that thing—over and over again—'til pastor had to lead her away."

"Bunny," Beryl learned, was the nickname for the baby of the family, Viola Mae. "D-boy," she now knew, was her father's.

"That's me!" Beryl exclaimed when Aunt Cleo turned to a page with littler Beryls and Randys.

As Aunt Cleo flipped through album after album, Beryl saw Nelsons being babies, being her age, getting married, grown old, and many dead in dark, wood caskets. Aunt Cleo had a story about every photo it seemed: the setting, the before and after events, and whatnot. She had the least to say about Uncle Lemuel. How odd, seeing as how there were so many photographs of him. In knickers. Being baptized. Singing in the choir. Graduating from high school. Graduating from college. Graduating from something again. Shaking hands with some important-looking white man. Sitting at a huge desk with lots of awards on the wall behind.

He was her father's mother's brother, Beryl learned—he with the long face and the teeny eyes, and always so serious, even as a child. From the little Aunt Cleo said, Beryl discovered that he was the family genius. "But no matter how high he rose, he was never out of reach," Aunt Cleo remembered. "Never knew a time when one of us had a problem and he couldn't help, whether it was with money so Dorothea and Bernice could finish their schooling, or cooling Kathleen's heels when she stomped off from her husband—and Uncle Lem was right. That George was a *good* man, and Kathleen sure was lucky he took her back. And, D-boy, you remember how he used to bring us peanuts and oranges every Saturday? Uncle Lem . . . always giving, always listening without a word of scorn whenever you needed a good talk-out."

Uncle Lemuel must have died a long time ago because after awhile when they came to his long face, the most Aunt Cleo might say was "And that's Uncle Lem, of course." But she didn't have a picture of him in a dark, wood casket.

"D-boy, Uncle Lem ought to be up by now. Why don't you and Ruth take him his plate?"

Beryl and her parents were in the kitchen keeping Aunt Cleo company while she did some food work. Uncle Jesse was on an errand, and Randy still wasn't back.

"Uncle Lem's sleeping 'til midday these days?" Mr. Nelson frowned.

"No, he still gets up way before day, but then rests his eyes around midmorning. Still likes to take his one meal a day out in the sun, weather permitting."

"Uncle Lemuel's not dead?" Beryl asked.

"No, baby," Aunt Cleo smiled. "He lives in the little house out back."

Beryl had noticed it on her way to the woods but had figured it was a tool shed or a garage, or what did it matter once she'd spotted the pond with ducks gliding around.

"Can I come?"

"Let them go alone this time," Aunt Cleo answered. "Been years since they've laid eyes on one another and, well, Uncle Lem's uneasy about meeting a lot of new people at once."

Beryl stood in the back door and watched her parents walk to the little house. It wasn't long after Mr. Nelson knocked that Uncle Lemuel emerged, with a card table and folding chair. Beryl saw them talking as Uncle Lemuel set up the table. Her father's mouth was moving more than his uncle's. Her mother's mouth just stayed in a smile.

"Why he lives out there?" Beryl asked Aunt Cleo.

"Oh, Uncle Lem is . . . well, let's just say he prefers to keep company with his thoughts."

Uncle Lemuel's face seemed shorter now that he had a long gray beard, which made her think of the movie she'd seen about Moses. She zeroed in on the part when he came down from his talk with God on the mountain clutching the Ten Commandments. He was glowing, and looking like he knew *everything* about *everybody*.

And Beryl determined in her mind that she'd get a closer look at this very distant relative, this Moses of the family.

But for right now and the rest of the day it'd be other people, people, people in a very up-close, loud, and almost dizzying way. As family poured in from due East, West, and farther Down South, Aunt Cleo's was mostly everybody's first stop, where folk sat and rested a bit, waiting for whoever was putting them up to pick them up. Most of Mr. Nelson's sisters and brothers lived fairly close by. Some had lots of room; others were just quick and learned in the ways of make-do. So cots had been set up in living rooms and basement corners. Pull-out couches and two-seaters were prepped. Bedrooms for two were made ready to sleep four. Plus, Aunt Cleo had a few friends on standby ready to lay out their welcome mat for any unexpecteds in the Nelson clan. Beryl's family was the only one staying with Aunt Cleo. She had room for more, but since hers was the site of Saturday's big-bash barbecue, her house would need a lot of rest.

The spread? Anyone could have guessed it'd be grand. This was, after all, a celebration. There were dozens of short and long tables spaced out around the backyard, all heavy laden with too much food, from large punch bowls of potato salad and field peas to wide pans of candied yams and macaroni and cheese. And tossed salad too? Beryl puzzled, because it seemed so puny next to all the other stuff, especially the tin-foiled trays of ribs and chicken and hot dogs and burgers and chopped barbecue, and the huge soup pots of greens—collards and turnips and mustards. Oh yuck! Beryl thought at the sight of the last two. But that high-rise cornbread she knew she could eat for days, just like she could that enormous coconut cake, ringed by half a dozen sweet potato pies. And there was peach ice cream that Uncle Jesse had made in his churn.

Beryl figured there wouldn't be too much left over for tomorrow, not with all these people. At this point she'd counted thirty-nine she called "Uncle," forty-seven she called "Aunt," and another fifty-four who were cousins, from little ones to some her parents' age. She wanted to break it down to see how many were first cousins versus seconds, and who-all in the crowd would call her grandniece, or great-grandniece, or great-great-grand-niece. She was starting in on this when she heard the quick beeps from a short string of cars, out of which more people were in a minute piling out.

After awhile, Mr. Nelson's oldest brother, Roy, called for quiet. He called for grace. "Heavenly Father, our heads are bowed, our minds are still. And we praise you . . . And we offer you thanks for this bounty, for the safe travels of our loved ones, and for the breath of life with which we pray for your ongoing guidance and mercy. We ask this in the name of Jesus Christ."

Every voice lifted up an "Amen," and it was as if they were a world, and there could be no wars. Mostly everybody was a Nelson and everybody else belonged to somebody who belonged to the Nelson family. So everybody belonged.

Very soon there was no more quiet. But it was not noise, for love sounds sweet.

And Beryl got plenty of it, in the form of cheek-tweaks, and swing-and-sway hugs, and so many questions—same ones over and over again, so much so that she wished she had a sign that read, "I'm ten years old, I'm in the fifth grade, and yes, I'm a good girl."

And who did this Cousin Mikey think he was, talking about how come *she* talks funny?

"And don't you look like your daddy spit you out!" every other grown-up exclaimed.

Beryl tensed up if Randy was close by when someone said that. She wondered if the whole family knew why Randy didn't look like her father. She started thinking back over the last day and a half and looking around now to see how people were treating Randy. No different than they treated her, she had to admit. They hugged and kissed and squeezed them the same. But it did seem as if they asked Randy more questions. Everybody kept saying how Randy was so smart, and going "Oooh," or "Well, well," when she told them she was going to be a poet, but giving Beryl a weak smile

124

or a flat "That's nice" when she said she was going to be a movie star.

Could it be that they all liked Randy more than her? She was more family to them. Wouldn't they . . . shouldn't they love her the best?

Why was it still scratching at her mind? Beryl wanted to let it go, like Grandma had said. She wanted to not worry about Randy being mad at her forever and leaving them, but . . . But maybe Uncle Lemuel could help?

He was outside now, sitting at his card table, which Aunt Cleo had dressed up pretty with a red and white checkered tablecloth. Beryl had seen some family send him smiles and waves from a distance. Every now and again she saw no more than two at a time go over to him and chat for awhile. As they walked back to the crowd, Beryl thought they looked different: something like wiser, something like the way people looked when they came from talking serious with a preacher. As old as he is, Beryl figured, Uncle Lemuel must have *a lot* of answers to a lot of problems. The closer she got, the older he looked, the wiser he seemed.

"Hi, sir, Uncle Lemuel," Beryl called out as she approached his table. "I'm Beryl. I'm your nephew Daniel's daughter, so I'm your great-niece, or something like that."

"Beryl . . .?" It was as if he were tasting her name. "A gemstone . . . precious." His smile was a hug. "Are you living up to your name?"

"I guess so." How could such little eyes seem so roomy, Beryl wondered as she stared at Uncle Lemuel as he just stared back. His eyes, though, didn't pierce.

She didn't know what she wanted to say.

She didn't know if she should say anything.

She didn't know how to begin.

"You seem troubled. What ails?" he asked.

"Nothing. I just wanted to say hey and ask you . . . Uncle Lemuel, make pretend you've been growing up all your life with a sister, but then you find out that she's not your whole sister. Would that bother you?"

"No. But then I don't care for botheration."

"Well, make pretend your sister was going to go visit her real father, would you be silly to be afraid she'll want to go live with him?"

"Perfect love casts out fear."

"Yeah, okay, but . . . Uncle Lemuel, do you know that my daddy isn't Randy's real father?"

Beryl watched his eyes roam to the sky. "I see . . . I see," he nodded.

To Beryl it seemed that he really did see. Everything. And understood her. "Everybody keeps telling me it don't make no difference and how I'm being—" Beryl broke off because Uncle Lemuel had closed his eyes. He must be getting wised up, she thought.

"Nice day." Uncle Lemuel's eyes were open now. "And what might your name be, my child?"

"It's Beryl, sir."

"And whose child might you be, little Miss Meryl?"

"No, it's *Beryl*."

"Sounds familiar. You look it, too." After a pause he questioned, "And who did you say your people are?"

"You my people, Uncle Lemuel. Remember I told you I'm Daniel's daughter?"

"Daniel?"

Beryl pointed at her father. "Yeah, but you probably call him D-boy."

"Hmmm, decent-looking young man. Even looks a little familiar."

"Uncle Lem—"

"Just a minute," he whispered. Then from his vest pocket he pulled out a gold watch, long chain trailing. He stared at the watch face intently for a good little while. And so did Beryl, for the watch had no hands.

"Ohmigoodness," Beryl said to herself as she began to back away from Uncle Lemuel. "We've got a crazyman in the family and no one even told me!"

"Hey, dumplin'!"

Beryl had backed into Aunt Bunny, all gussied up in hot pink and ruffles. When Beryl met her yesterday, she had taken a big fancy to her, and to her chewing gum and bangles. Aunt Cleo she loved a lot, but Aunt Bunny was fun.

"Been visiting with Uncle Lem? Ain't that nice?" twittered Aunt Bunny.

"Yeah, but—"

"Why you looking like you seen a ghost?" Aunt Bunny didn't stay still for an answer, but kept on stepping in her high-heeled silvery shoes over to Uncle Lemuel to give him the plate of food she had in her hand.

Beryl watched, rooted in the same spot. When Aunt Bunny returned her way, she whispered, "I didn't know Uncle Lemuel was a crazyman."

"Dumplin', don't call him that. He . . . he had a, an accident many years ago, and it left him a little . . . changed. So sometimes Uncle Lem talks strange while other times he talks the same sense he always did. He say something to scare you?"

"No. I was just asking . . . Aunt Bunny, do you know that my daddy ain't Randy's real father?"

" 'Course I do."

Beryl was stunned by Aunt Bunny's so-quick-and-easy answer. "How long you known?"

"Ever since the time he brought your mama and Randy down here to—uh-uh, no I'm wrong, I take that back, because when D-boy met your mama he was just bragging away long-distance, told us everything about this dreamboat he'd met, and so naturally we knew she had a daughter, but it wasn't 'til he brought both of them down here to visit that we knew for sure we were going to have ourselves a new niece!"

"So everybody in the whole family knew from the beginning?"

128

"Everybody who wasn't dead, I suppose . . . And just as cute as spring she was, the way your mama had her all dolled up in this satin and lace little white dress and— Can you keep a secret?"

Braced for another shock, Beryl nodded.

"When you come by my house I'll show you that picture of your mama and Randy when they were down here. I snuck it from Cleo."

"So nobody minded?"

"You can bet Cleo minded something terrible."

"No, I mean that my mother had a—that Randy wasn't—that, you know . . ."

"Ohh, I think I'm seeing what you're meaning," whispered Aunt Bunny. Voice normal again, and one hand on her hip, she continued, "Dumplin', why in the world would anybody in their right mind have minded? Far as we were all concerned, your mama was the best thing that ever happened to your daddy, for he was a rather trifling sort, if I must say so myself, but not after he got a-hold of your mama, because it was like he became a new man."

Aunt Bunny punctuated her pronouncement with a hard nod of her head. Before Beryl could even think of getting a word in edgewise, Aunt Bunny was talking again. "What I'm getting at is that we all came to love your mother, so how could we not love her child? Didn't make us no never mind how she come to be one of us. All it meant was the family was bigger by two. Just like when you came along we couldn't help but love you too."

"You love me and Randy the same? Even though she's really only my half-sister, which makes you like a half-aunt or something?"

"Half?" Aunt Bunny frowned. "Beryl, it's not the blood. It's the love. And that's one thing I'm a living witness of." She gave Beryl's chin a little squeeze and shake. "And ain't family a funny thing? Sometimes I forget how some people come to be family—whether they was born into it, married into, or just showed up one day. All I know is that they're . . . just family. Like I was saying, to me when D-boy got married I got a new sister. Or like you take Cousin 'Neatha— You met her yet?"

Beryl shook her head, too dizzy from Aunt Bunny's talk to talk herself.

"Well, you will," Aunt Bunny said as she surveyed the crowd, before speeding on with "and she ain't our blood cousin. Our mamas was best friends from the time they were seven until the day they died three days apart at the age of sixty-four—both of them. It was so uncanny. As much as they loved each other, as close as those two women were, they might as well have been sisters, so naturally that makes their children cousins, and so that's how 'Neatha is my cousin, and how her little boy, Mikey, is your second cousin."

Mikey, I've met, Beryl said to herself.

"And I'll give you another for instance in Bessie who everybody say I favor so much. And I do, only I think it's more in ways than in looks, but we could pass for sisters or first cousins, I do think, but you see, she was married to Cousin Horace, until he got tangle-headed and ran off with one of those shimmy girls from down Thompson Creek way, and then 'generated into a real pig. But you know, everybody loved Bessie so much, she just kinda took his place in our hearts—not that we disown Horace or nothing, though 'tis true we don't hardly call his name without spitting, and we do keep our distance—whereas Bessie who ain't even got a child from the man as a sort of passport to the family, she feels more like closer kin than he do. Then, there's—

"Beryl! . . . Beryl!"

Without looking over her shoulder Beryl knew who that somebody was who was calling her name. Now that they'd made eye contact, Mrs. Nelson was waving her to join her and Mr. Nelson, standing opposite the widest woman Beryl had ever seen in her life. And way taller than Aunt Cleo.

"Better run along," said Aunt Bunny. "We'll talk some more later."

12

That lady must can't fit through the door of a regular house, Beryl thought as she made her way to her parents. As she drew closer, she sighed. And if she hit you with those hams she's got for hands, you'll be dead for sure. My goodness, Beryl shook her head, this family's got some of everything: a crazyman, a motor-mouth, a giant.

As she came closer, she saw Randy approaching her parents. By the time Beryl reached her father's side, he already had one arm around Randy's shoulder and was waiting to drape the other around hers.

"This here's our oldest, Randy," said Mr. Nelson. "And this here is the baby, Beryl." Then turning his head to each, he said, "Randy, Beryl, this is Cousin Tiny."

Beryl and Randy were so glad when their parents started talking old times with Cousin Tiny. They couldn't wait to get away and let loose their laughter, and get silly.

They dashed behind one of the black-bark walnut trees on the edge of Aunt Cleo and Uncle Jesse's property, and plopped down to giggle under its canopy of long yellow-green leaves. When they got through laughing about Cousin Tiny, they found other things to snicker about.

Like the man whose name they couldn't remember so they called him "Uncle Drunk."

"Did you see when Aunt Cleo snatched his bottle and poured his liquor on the ground?" Randy whispered.

Like Aunt Sarah's teeth falling into the potato salad, and Cousin Casper falling off the log and into the pond when he was trying to play Fred Astaire.

"That's what he gets for trying to show off," Beryl giggled.

"You shouldn't be laughing," Randy teased, "seeing as how last night you fell out of the bed just trying to sleep!" Randy had a good laugh behind that. Then, seeing that Beryl had drawn a blank she asked, "You don't remember?"

The tumble out of bed . . . the feeling of warm and safe. This morning, she had recalled it all as a dream. "That was you?"

"No, it was Mr. Magoo," Randy laughed. Beryl still wasn't laughing, but that changed soon as they got back to some of the scenes and puzzlements of their Down South days.

Like the so many Bobbys in the family.

"Little Bobby, Big Bobby, Bobby Lee," Beryl counted.

"And there's the one they call 'Blue,' " Randy added. "And there's Jimmy's sister, only she spells her name with an i-e."

"Who's Jimmy's parents?" Beryl asked.

"He's Uncle Jesse's sister's son," answered Randy, peeping around the side of the tree. "I don't see his mother, but see that man by the barbecue pit, with the blue shirt? That's his father."

Slouched across Randy's lap in a peeping posture, Beryl asked, "Who's that man standing next to him with the white shoes? He gave me a quarter."

"That's Uncle Riley. He's Aunt Bunny's brother."

"Aunt Bunny? Then he's Daddy's brother."

"Uh-uh," Randy corrected. "You don't know about Aunt Bunny?"

"Know what?!" Beryl sat up.

"Her mother was Daddy's mother's cousin."

"Huh?"

"Yeah. What happened was when she was a baby her house caught on fire, and she was the only one Uncle Riley was able to save. There was four of them, I think, not counting the parents. And Uncle Riley was almost a grown man, so he could live on his own. But Aunt Bunny . . . Daddy's parents took her in."

Beryl sat back against the tree. "How you know all this?"

"Daddy told me."

"When?"

"When we were driving down."

"Where was I?"

"You were asleep. It was when I was riding shotgun."

What-all else did everybody except her know about? "Well, have you met Uncle Lemuel? I have."

"Not yet."

"Aunt Bunny said I shouldn't call him a crazyman, but that's what I think he is."

"But it's a miracle he lived."

"What do you know about him?"

"I know about what those drunken rednecks did to him."

"Aunt Bunny said he had an accident."

Randy leaned in close. "That's not really what happened."

"It's not?" Beryl gasped.

"His car broke down one night, and outside of town. Some white men pulled up. He thought they were stopping to help him, but they started beating him up really bad and calling him 'Mr. Uppity.' Then they beat him some more and left him for dead."

All along, Down South had seemed to Beryl a perfect wonderland. "Who told you about this?"

"Daddy."

"When?"

"When we were driving down."

"Where was I?"

"You were—"

"Asleep?"

"Uh-huh."

"Well, I'm not sleeping on the way back home. I miss too much." Nothing was simple and neat, she was thinking. Everything had curves and different sides; nothing was plain smooth. "But, so, why'd Aunt Bunny say he had an accident?"

"Probably because she thought you were too young to handle such a sad story."

"I'm not, you know."

"I know, but you know how grown-ups are."

"Yeah," Beryl sighed. "Randy?"

"Yeah?"

"What do you call somebody you like who's a little crazy? Is lunatic a bad word?"

"Beryl, just call him Uncle Lemuel."

"Maybe if I get to talk to him again I'll ask if I can say Lem, like everybody else." After a small silence, Beryl asked, "What's a redneck?"

"Well, it's what black people down here call the white people who are mean and nasty to them."

"When did this happen to Uncle Lemuel?"

"It was a long, long time ago. In the 1950s, I think."

"They still have rednecks down here?"

"Probably."

"Their necks really red?"

Randy gave Beryl a playful shove. "Of course not,

silly!" Her laughter helped Beryl ease up on her feeling of fear.

"Randy?"

"Yeah?"

"Are we gossiping, talking about Aunt Bunny and Uncle Lemuel like this?"

"No, we're just talking. Besides, we're sisters so we can talk about stuff like this. And it's our family. It's not like we're saying anything that's not true. Gossiping would be like if I said I heard that Cousin Tiny sleeps with no clothes on or something."

"She *does*?"

"No! I'm saying that would be like gossip, and if you went and told somebody else without knowing whether it was true or not you'd be making more gossip. But I guess even if you knew it was true, it's probably wrong to be telling people about something like that."

"Huh?"

"Never mind."

It was nearing sundown. There was still a lot of talking and cutting up, and eating going on, but you could hear folks winding down a bit, along with the day. There was more low-talk, fewer outbursts of loud, contagious, ringing laughter. And now that everyone had had their fill of being so glad to see each other, there were bits of bicker and clips of petty jealousies, along with the sighs of frayed nerves in the background, and old grudges were trotting out. As day follows night, the reunion was drawing out the best in many and the worst in some.

When Beryl peeped around the tree trunk, she saw no swell of people around the tables of food, and no new faces in the crowd. She spotted her parents strolling over to the woods, holding hands. She eased back against the tree. "Randy, you know, I don't think Ma's going to have any more children."

"So."

"So what I mean is, how you feel about me being the only sister you ever have for your who-o-ole life?"

"Depends on if you're gonna be a whiner your who-o-ole life."

"I whine a lot?"

Randy rolled her eyes bigtime. "And you're nosy and pesty, too, you know."

"I thought it was good to be curious. Mrs. Pellegrino said it was how we learn. And Grandma said it's good to question."

"But there's a difference between being good curious and pain-in-the-butt curious."

"What's the difference?"

"Well . . ." Randy said slowly, trying to think fast. "I guess you know it's the okay kind if you don't get on anybody's nerves."

"I get on your nerves a lot?"

"Yeah!" Randy said with gusto. Then the wash of hurt

on Beryl's face moved her to add, "But like Ma and Daddy are always saying, you'll grow out of it."

"I will?"

"They say I did."

"You used to get on people's nerves when you were a kid?"

"That's what they say."

"You know, Linda says I'm lucky to have a big sister. Anybody ever tell you you're lucky to have a little sister?"

"No."

"Oh." Beryl looked down at the grass and noticed how it almost matched her pedal pushers. Tomorrow she'd wear the ones that looked like the sky. "I'm real sorry I called you that name. I won't ever, ever, ever say it again." She could feel Randy's eyes on her face. "I'm not even gonna think that way no more." She was tempted to sneak a peek up at Randy.

"Thanks."

Beryl turned to her. "This mean you unmad at me?"

"Yeah."

"For good? Forever?"

"That's gonna depend on how you act."

Oh, boy. Beryl's sigh was a big one. She didn't take offense when Randy laughed. She wanted to laugh, too, now. Being good wasn't funny, though. She couldn't imagine being good forever. How could anyone do that?

Especially since you couldn't always tell when you were getting ready to be bad.

"You know, Ma and Daddy say I used to get into everything just like you, and anytime I heard them talking about someone I'd say, 'Who? Who?' They say I used to ask a *lot* of questions, at the wrong time, mostly. And they say I used to talk, and talk, and talk, and . . .

Randy and Beryl sat there awhile longer and talked and talked and talked.

"So what stuff were you doing when Cousin Jimmy took you around?" was how Beryl had kicked up a new exchange.

13

During the rest of the family's nine days in Greenwood, South Carolina, things got back to normal in Beryl's mind. Maybe it was the talking and sharing with Randy. When she searched around for the anger and disappointment at her mother, Beryl found not a twinge. Something had changed as everything went back to the same.

Maybe it was just a matter of time—in this case, time made marvelous with so many things Beryl would always remember. Those nighttime back-porch stories that began "Hey, D-boy, 'member the time . . ." Those drives around town to see where Mr. Nelson's school used to be, and the house in which he grew up. Those visits with folks he'd grown up with, and that old, old lady who said she'd "known him 'fore he was born." That crazy afternoon at Aunt Bunny's house, playing dress-up and dancing around in her pointy-toed spike-heel shoes. And there was the day Uncle Jesse and Uncle

Roy took them fishing, and Beryl got to tease Randy for a change, so squeamy she was about worming her hook. For Beryl it was a kick. She didn't catch catfish one, but she sure had a good time baiting up.

And then, there was that next to the last Down South day, a laze-around day—and her last conversation with Uncle Lemuel.

Beryl and Randy had taken him his meal a few afternoons. He'd seemed to like it when they sat down and talked with him awhile. He'd talk clear one moment about the land, or things he'd read about in books, or lived. There were sketchy stories about some of his long-ago students who became important people. A few times, he'd just sit quiet, and they'd just as quietly leave. Other times, no matter what the conversation, he'd pause, look beyond them, and there'd be a switch to talk that was pretty, but so strange. At him, Beryl and Randy never laughed.

This time Beryl had come alone, and this time he was talking about trees.

"*Nyssa sylvatica* is the Latin name for what we call Black Gum . . . *Prunus caroliniana* we know as Cherry Laurel . . . *Fraxinus* we call an Ash."

"I saw a movie about a man named Spartacus," Beryl piped up. "That a tree's name?"

Had he heard her? She didn't know. He just kept on pointing out the trees. "*Quercus*. Now don't that sound like an oak? And over there next to that skinny, skinny thing is *Acer saccharum*, a Maple, only I've named that one a Cleo tree."

"After Aunt Cleo?"

"At the same time strong and sweet. Cleo told me to live when I wanted to die. So I gave her a tree. Would you like a tree?"

"I'm going home tomorrow, Uncle Lem."

"Home?"

"New York."

"You can still have a tree."

"But I don't know when I'm coming back down here. I may never see it again after tomorrow."

"Need you see it for it to be real?"

"I guess not." And at that moment she felt he was talking sense. "I'll have a tree," she smiled.

"See that there one to the right of the Cleo tree?"

"That little bush?" Beryl frowned.

"Yes, indeed. But one day it'll be a tall, tall . . ."

Next to her father, Beryl named Uncle Lemuel the most wonderful man in the world. "You got a tree for Randy?" Struck worried by Uncle Lemuel's puzzled gaze, she added, "My sister, remember we—"

"I know who she is. Just not sure what tree she'll be," Uncle Lemuel responded. "A willow most likely. *Salix.* And there's one way, way over yonder," he said, pointing in the direction of the woods.

———

143

And it was there that Beryl allowed herself to wander after she said good-bye to Uncle Lemuel, hugging him for the first time.

It was dusk. Poised for the shift from day to night, the sky had that soft-light glow, colored blue edging powder rose edging almost gold, and looking like it was ready to whisper safe secrets.

Cric.

Ket.

Cric.

Ket.

Cricket-Cricket.

Twigs snapping told Beryl that small animals were in motion, scampering, scooting, darting about, but she felt no dread. She was caught up in listening and watching what the wind was doing to the trees. Still, calmly still, she was standing, not knowing why, not even aware that this was the first time she'd ever *wanted* to be alone.

And there came to her remembrance, in leaps and spins, the questions, the thoughts, and all the conversations that had boiled up from her finding out about that Rusty man.

It wasn't simple sadness she was feeling. This was something else. It was sorry. But not the sorry sparked by fear. It would be a few years before she'd be able to name these feelings. Regret. Shame. No, she didn't feel bad about wanting to know the truth. In that pure, clear, unbeginning and quiet part of her being, she knew she had not been wrong. Her behavior, though, had been not so good she was sure.

Beryl never would come up with quite the right word for this other feeling rising up in her now, guiding her attention away from the regret, the shame, and on to something beyond. It was a feeling of . . .

Was this what the sun felt like when it was trying to break through the clouds?

"Dear God," she heard herself whisper. "I'm sorry I got on everybody's nerves. You're holy and, probably, you don't have nerves, but if you do and I got on them, then I'm saying sorry to you, too. Please make me better. Send a message to everybody's heart that it was just that I was trying to understand, and I was scared, and that I love them. Ma . . . Daddy . . . Randy—" Beryl broke off because an idea had burst in. She raced to the house and in search of some paper.

"Why aren't we leaving when it's night?"

"Heavier traffic the farther North we get. But it'll be less at night. Besides, the South has prettier sights."

The strong embraces and handshake-hugs and kisses had finally come to an end. Of the family who'd come to see them off, some were now milling around the front yard, others making their way to the porch, and a few were pulling off to go to or get back to work.

Aunt Cleo and Mrs. Nelson were by the front of the

car having a last talk. Randy was making her way down the porch steps, delighting over the picture postcards of South Carolina, which Cousin Jimmy had promised he'd get and had just delivered. Beryl had gotten last tag on Cousin Mikey just as his mother called him into the house, and she couldn't think of anything better to do than watch her father pack their luggage in the trunk.

"Are we ever coming back down here?"

"Matter of fact, last night Aunt Cleo was saying how she'd love for you and Randy to come down next year and stay the whole summer. Randy said she'd love to."

"Where was—I mean . . . That'd be fun, Daddy. Can we?"

Mr. Nelson nodded that, yes, they probably could. When he closed the trunk, Beryl skipped to the passenger side front door, but stopped short of getting in. "Randy? You want to ride shotgun now?"

"Nah, I want the night shift."

"Ma, you want to sit up front?"

"Only if you don't want to."

"I went first on the way down."

Once all were inside, they gave Aunt Cleo and Uncle Jesse and the small crowd of remaining kin a so-long wave.

"Be sure to call when you get home," hollered Aunt Cleo.

"We will," Mrs. Nelson hollered back.

The car started up and after a quick farewell beep-beep, Beryl and her family were gone.

Along small streets that would take them to a wide road. Passing by houses with lots of land, and silos, and water tanks, and lone, leaning sheds. Passing by farmed land and signs for bushels of fruits and vegetables. Passing by stretches of close-together batches of trees belonging to no one. Passing by more and more cars and pickup trucks and a traffic light.

By and by they met up with the highway with its sleek, flat, smooth self. And if it could talk, it would grin and say, "Better get a move on!"

And now Mr. Nelson is driving faster, elbow resting where the window would be if it weren't down because it is hot! But Mr. Nelson doesn't believe in air-conditioning, not on his parting ride through his bit of Down South. They are all enjoying the hot breeze.

The Nelson family is glad to be going home, but nobody is glad to be leaving. It is too early to talk about all they've just said good-bye to, and too early to think about the city life they'll soon be back into.

They are in a pause, in a linger state of mind and mood. They are far enough along the road home to know that if any of them has left anything at Aunt Cleo's house, it's way too late to turn back.

Beryl has been waiting for this moment, a right moment.

So now she draws a piece of paper, folded small, from her back pocket, and now she clears her throat.

"I have something I—I wrote something I'd like y'all to hear. I named it 'So Sorry.'" Again she clears her throat, and in her best church program voice, spiked by quick breaths, she reads:

> i know sometimes i'm a pain.
> and i make EVERYBODY
> insane
> i whine a lot.
> and it's MY fault my head got a knot.
> BUT
> i want you to know
> that i love u so-o-o-oo
> MUCH!
> and God's not through with me yet.

Beryl wasn't exactly expecting applause, but she sure was hoping that somebody would say something.

"That's all I wrote," she said in a small voice.

"Oh!" cried Mrs. Nelson. "It was going so beautiful, I was just waiting for more."

"Short and sweet, popcorn," said Mr. Nelson. "Sounds like you've been doing some thinking."

"Uh-huh. And I—"

"Lemme see that," Randy broke in.

Beryl hesitated, but then handed Randy her poem.

Randy looked it over quickly, and then twice more. "So-o-o," she finally spoke with some clip to her tone, "why didn't you just write it straight, Beryl? And why didn't you start every line with a capital letter?"

"You like it?"

"Pretty good," Randy nodded, a broad smile now. "Pretty good."

Beryl was all sunbeams and peace as she and her family continued on their journey home.

And so . . .

Did Beryl continue to be less contrary? Yes! Only sometimes
it was, No. Like when the day came for Randy to meet
Rusty, and Beryl couldn't go. Maybe if there's a next time,
her parents left her to hope. But she didn't mope for long,
not with Grandma there with ginger ale and popcorn, too,
and game upon game of Rummy 500—with
her South Carolina souvenir.
When Randy returned . . . What was he like? Beryl was in
a hurry to know. But she'd made a vow not to be so bold,
and gave Randy room to share, and she didn't care if Randy
went again, right then, to Philly. She knew her sister wasn't
going anywhere. Of course, it helped to know that
the man wasn't rich. And by summer's end,
Beryl had mastered the alligator stitch.

11198